Summer Devon

D1743139

This book is a work of fiction. The names, characters, places, and incidents are products of the writer's imagination. Any resemblance to persons, living or dead, actual events, locale or organizations is entirely coincidental.

Dedication

For L.B. Gregg, Eli Easton, K.A. Mitchell, Liv Rancourt, and Bonnie Dee: their stories are just what the doctor ordered.

Also to Lori Fritts in case she actually carries through on her threat and reads one of my books.

His Scottish Detective

Summer Devon

2018

His Scottish Detective

Summer Devon

Chapter One

London, 1886

A truncheon swooped through the air. Joshua ducked—and good thing he did. The club would have smashed his head. He should have stopped moving, though.

His first mistake had been coming to the house. The second and far worse mistake came that moment after he avoided the truncheon. If he'd been using his brain, he would have gone utterly still except to raise his hands in surrender.

Instead, years of training lurched into his body, and he grabbed the stick, yanked it away, swept the bloke's legs out from under him, and was about to use the stick on the attacker's own noggin when Joshua came back to thinking. He dropped the damned weapon.

Too late, because the man who'd been holding the truncheon was a peeler. Joshua might have taken care of a single man, but the stick wielder hadn't led the raid on the molly house alone. His friends and about a dozen fellow coppers landed on Joshua with shouts and blows. One voice yelled above the rest, and, just before he passed out, Joshua heard, "Enough. There's no need to kill the poor fool."

By the time Joshua regained consciousness, he knew two things. He was lying on the floor of a jail cell, and no way on earth would he tell them his real name, though he wasn't sure he could talk. His jaw and throat blazed with pain, and he didn't want to attempt to open his mouth. When he shifted slightly, his leg and hip seemed to be stabbed with something sharp, he could swear it. Nearby, other men whimpered and shouted.

Apparently, all the molly house occupants had gotten a proper drubbing. Joshua had a passing hope that the police response wasn't due to his own wrong move. The whole thing hardly seemed fair. He'd been in the place less than ten minutes. Unfair since others shouldn't suffer because of his bad response, and as for himself, he didn't even have the satisfaction of finally touching another man.

Someone prodded his shoulder. "This one is hurt badly."

He grunted.

"He resisted arrest, attacked an officer."

"For those sins, he shouldn't die," the first one said again. He had a peculiar accent. Irish maybe. It was the man who'd yelled during the attack and called Joshua a poor fool.

The description of fool fit, though Joshua didn't care about that. When he tried to move, he once again blacked out, not so very long this time. When he woke again, he was still on the floor. Someone had shoved him to the side and was going through his pockets. The cold of the cell registered, but the pain of his legs, throat, and head made a greater clamor for his attention. He passed out again.

The next time he noticed his surroundings, he decided the breeze crossing his skin meant his coat and waistcoat were gone. His shirt was ripped. His throat felt as if it had been slashed, and he had trouble drawing breath.

"He's near dead," someone near his head spoke.

They were speaking of him. Joshua waited to feel sad, but death was a better choice just now.

The pain would cease, and he wouldn't have to face his father.

If there was one thing Big Mervin didn't tolerate, it was a man who let himself get caught by the police. He also didn't think much of frailty or imperfection, or a man who lusted for men instead of women.

His father's list of "transgrassons," as he called them, was long and, if too many items on it were ticked off, you were done.

Nicky had been too kind, too sweet, too blundering, and ended up dead in the Thames.

And was that Nicky grabbing Joshua now? He started awake as his brother tried to pull his leg off or pull him under the water. "No! No! Gerroff, Nick," he said.

"I'm already in trouble for your sake, idiot. They won't get the surgeon in here," someone said. The man with the accent again. "Here, you." The pain lessened as the man let go of Joshua's foot. "Mike, that your name?" *No, Joshua*, he almost answered, then realized the officer was talking to the other prisoner. The man with authority continued talking. "Right. Hold tight while I get this bone back where it belongs."

And then the agony roared back to life again far worse.

That's done it, Joshua decided. He couldn't survive that, thank bloody hell.

The next time he woke entirely, he had an actual blanket over him and the pain throbbed rather than stabbed and had diminished enough to allow him to think. His mouth was dry and tasted of rotten meat and old copper, but he recalled someone giving him water and broth, more than once.

Not Nicky, he thought with a wash of sorrow. He opened his eyes and looked around the small dingy cell. His gaze landed on a large grizzled man in rumpled workman's clothes standing near him, looking down at him.

"You're awake? Budge down." The man, nearly as big as Joshua himself, waited patiently until Joshua gingerly inched down the hard bench, the only furniture in the cell. The man looked familiar—he might have been the doorman from the molly house.

With a grunt and a sigh, the big man sat again. "I'm Mike," he said.

"Thank you for taking care of me," Joshua rasped. His throat wouldn't work right.

"I ain't done much more than feed you broth like the man told me to."

"Man?"

"The crusher. Munro. Sergeant maybe? Fairly new round here. New to London. I only seen him once before." The big man shook out a newspaper and turned the pages. For a few minutes, the scene felt almost homey. Joshua hadn't known they allowed newspapers in prison. They were in Newgate, he decided. Not as bad as Millbank, the only other prison he'd seen—the place his mother had ended up, a dank marsh of a place on the Thames.

He dozed and woke again at something clanking. He kept his eyes shut.

"What happens to us?" He could barely speak. It was as if someone stood on his throat. Was it a boot that had ruined his voice?

"If you'd kindly give me your name, we shall proceed from there." There was that lilt again, which didn't work with the cop's attempt to sound tough.

Joshua leaned his head to the side to look around. The other prisoner was gone. Only one other person was in the cell with him, a lean figure in a suit. Though he wasn't in a uniform, the way he stood, straight and sneering, screamed police. And there was the peculiar accent.

"Munro? Sergeant?" Joshua whispered.

Munro stared back without a trace of humor on his face or his light eyes. Gray? Blue? Joshua couldn't see details, but he knew this man was definitely a crusher. "That's me identified. Now there's the matter of you."

Joshua considered lying, but by now, someone from the jail would have told, who would have told someone else, who would have told Big Mervin. Joshua would live, sad enough, and music would have to be faced. His plan to examine other paths in life, like his plans to touch another man, were at an end.

"Smith," he croaked.

"Pull the other one." Munro sounded disgusted. "I never met so many Smiths and Joneses in my life until we raided that house."

Joshua couldn't help it, he laughed, and that air rushing in his throat hurt so much, he stopped at once.

He pointed at his neck. "Something's wrong."

"Your leg was bad enough we didn't bother about your throat." Munro narrowed his eyes, which were icy gray or blue. Cold as the wind across the prison's stone floor. "Hurts, eh?"

Joshua nodded. He tried again. "Smith. Is. My. Name."

The briefest of smiles flitted across Munro's face. Mocking or not, the expression made him look nearly human. "Well then, Mr. Smith. I choose to believe you since it took so much effort to say as much. No, don't try to speak again." His smile grew to show teeth, white with a slightly crooked one at the side. "Must be hell going through life with that as a name. Don't die on us, eh? Not after Mike and I went through the bother of keeping you alive. I've had the devil of a time because of you."

He sounded more like regular gentry now, and Joshua wondered if he'd imagined the accent.

Joshua closed his eyes and tried to listen but instead he fell asleep, nearly like passing out, but with more frightening dreams.

The next time he woke, Mr. McLeevy, his father's lawyer, stood over him, and he suspected the real nightmare would now commence.

"I've already spoken to witnesses." McLeevy wiped his face with a handkerchief. He was a red sort of man, with a bulky frame without an ounce of real strength in it. He flushed red and sweated all the time, which made him look nervous. He'd once said it was why he was a solicitor and not barrister. "The bluebottles would have killed you if it weren't for one particular sergeant. And he's not even one of ours."

*One of our*s meant an officer bought and paid for by Big Mervin Smith, who handed out many guineas to keep himself and his associates out of the papers and prisons.

"Munro," Joshua whispered.

"That's the one I meant. You owe him your life." McLeevy's heavy gray eyebrows bunched in a worried frown. "Though what your father would say about owing one of them anything, I don't like to think. Best to leave it quiet."

Joshua nodded. He understood. This was a debt he'd have to pay back. In his world, there were few acts without retribution or repayment, depending.

On his return to the fold—arranged so the important authorities never knew whose son he was—it soon became clear Joshua's own value had decreased to nearly nil. He didn't think it was just the ill-fated trip to the molly house that pushed him to the edge of the organization. He'd had a bad attitude for a while, and now he was damaged goods.

Several months passed, and his body improved, though his status in the family remained uncertain. Even after he'd healed, he had a limp and his voice was changed forever—and ineffective workers didn't rate attention. He reckoned his limp and voice made him too memorable now to be pushed into any shadow of legit business.

His tumble off the ladder in the business wasn't personal, of course. It just wouldn't do to expend time or effort on any asset without some return for Big Mervin's time.

Joshua was told not to leave the warren. He managed to scrounge enough food to live on and made vague plans to flee the family, which would mean leaving London, probably. That idea, once it lit in his brain, seemed more interesting than anything else he'd conjured since Nicky's death.

His low status meant that Joshua didn't hear of his upcoming marriage directly from his father. McLeevy brought him the news that Joshua was to take a bride, the ceremony to be held in a fortnight.

"To stop the gossip about where I'd visited that night?" Joshua asked.

McLeevy actually winced and wrinkled his nose. "No one ever brought up where you were or why you were there. It's not germane to any family issues."

That was good, Joshua supposed.

The lawyer unfolded his handkerchief and wiped his temples. "The marriage is by way of a peacemaking, maybe negotiation. I'm not sure."

"Need to know," Joshua mumbled one of the family's mottos.

"Indeed." McLeevy tucked away his handkerchief. "But it's certainly a financial event."

"Oh?"

His worry must have shown on his face, because McLeevy hastily reassured him.

"No, no, you're in the clear. Her father is paying a pretty penny to get her married."

That made Joshua feel slightly better, because the ledger tilted in his favor. He didn't feel pride when he'd enriched the family coffers or guilt at depleting them. His response was only a measure of relief or apprehension. Everything in the Smith family was for sale. He rather hoped he'd fetched a good price.

He met his bride, a dark-haired woman of about twenty named Matilda, at the wedding in a small chapel not far from Piccadilly Square. It was a dismal affair with just the two of them and two witnesses who worked for his father and two witnesses from her family—the Neelys were a Smith rival he'd heard of. Big Mervin didn't come, but neither did her parents. She didn't speak except to repeat the vows. She didn't look at him or anyone else. The reason she'd had to be married was obvious right away. Her belly stuck out of her thin frame.

He didn't mind the whole event; after all, he had no one else he'd ever marry, but a spark of pity for the girl hit him. He wanted to ask about the baby's father and why she wouldn't marry him, but settled for "You all right, then?" But even at that small question, she shrank away. When he saw she had tears in her eyes, he gave up. Joshua knew he was threatening in appearance. That was an asset after all, a hulking man with big hands and now grinding stones for a voice.

She had a large satchel that she placed beside her during the short ceremony. Afterward, he offered to carry it.

"No!" She cringed away. Again.

There was no wedding breakfast, and within minutes, they went away together in a carriage driven by a man in her father's employment. Neely's man said he was to drive them to a small apartment that belonged to the newlyweds now.

In a low voice, Matilda admitted she'd never seen their new home. Through the ride, she clutched the satchel to her chest, resting it on her belly. Was it all she'd been allowed to take? Joshua didn't like the wave of pity that rushed through him at the thought.

"Her father's giving the place on the first story to you pair of sweethearts," the driver told them. The man, as plainly a heavy as any in Big Mervin's organization, saw them into the building.

"Have fun, lovebirds," he called after them. "Don't you bother coming out for at least a week. We left you plenty of provisions."

"Seem like a threat to you?" Joshua asked his new wife, but she cringed away from him. He climbed the stairs to the new apartment and discovered the place was unlocked.

Before Joshua could even tour the apartment with her, Matilda fled into a room and locked the door against him. She stayed hidden away there the rest of the night.

He tried calling to her, but the walls were thick enough she didn't hear him or didn't listen. On bad days, his voice only went above a whispering croak with effort. This was a bad day.

By noon the next day, he realized that even if she couldn't or wouldn't hear him, he could write her notes and push them under the door.

Don't worry. I won't hurt you, was the first thing he wrote to her—the first of many.

While he waited, he read books and examined the apartment, which had been decorated by someone with a taste for lace, feather shadowboxes, and colorful lamps. Presumably, Mr. Neely had used it for a female before he gave it to his daughter.

Eventually, Matilda came out of the room. She rushed into the kitchen and grabbed up some food—a bunch of uncooked carrots and a loaf of bread—then ran back into the room. He stayed back and wondered if he'd been married to a lunatic or feeble-minded creature. The high dowry would make some sense in that case.

He couldn't leave the apartment yet, so he continued to read books about accounting McLeevy had put into his luggage. Big Mervin had decided Joshua had brains and training enough to try that now that he was too damaged to go out to do proper family business. Maybe now that he had a wife, he'd stay put and do just that. He put aside his half-baked ideas of fleeing and he read.

Between dull pages, Joshua wrote notes to his bride, asking her questions. *Do you want a cup of tea? What do you like to do for entertainment? Do you like music?* He pushed the papers under the door and wedged a pencil under there as well.

She didn't answer them at first. Then she wrote: *I appreciate your effort to make me comfortable. Thank you.*

She had an educated hand and used fancy words spelled properly.

In late afternoon, he wrote another note telling her he was going out and saying he'd be back in three hours.

He had no particular desire to go anywhere—he supposed her family had someone watching the place, the same ones who dropped off groceries—but he'd give her solitude to recover without him there. The poor woman probably needed to bathe.

When he'd returned from dinner at a music hall, he found a letter from her telling him she'd taken all the money and jewelry she could find. She'd run away. She said she was very sorry, but she couldn't stay in London another day. She and her satchel were gone.

That was the end of his marriage…except it wasn't. A week later, he was rather shocked to find a longer letter from her apologizing for her flight. She had to go, but for reasons she couldn't divulge, she must stay away. She wouldn't shame him by telling anyone of their connection, she told him. *I am with a friend I trust who will help me.*

She begged him not to tell anyone where she'd gone, and it touched him that she trusted him to stay silent. Her handwriting was shaky, as if she were still afraid, and the last line was a hurried scrawl. *I'm sure you'd be a good husband to someone, and I hope you are not upset, but, at the moment I fled, I had no other answers. I still don't know what else I could have done.*

For some reason, he felt he couldn't just drop the whole event and pretend it never happened. And, because she provided a return address in care of an inn in Derbyshire, he wrote back and said he didn't mind and she should tell him if she needed anything. Only after he posted it did it occur to him that she would probably not be daft enough to send a final letter. She'd likely been stopping in Derbyshire on her way to another destination.

He had nowhere else in particular he wanted to go, so he stayed put in the apartment. Might as well cover for the girl as long as he could. He settled into life in the apartment alone with some relief at being out from under the daily tension of Big Mervin's organization.

Joshua sat in his empty apartment, paid for by Matilda's father, a man who hadn't attended his daughter's wedding.

Joshua found it cluttered and fussy yet comfortable. He found he liked soft furniture. And it was as good a place as any to wait before he'd be called back to duty again, after the month's honeymoon time he'd been allotted.

Matilda hadn't stolen much from Joshua. He'd had his billfold with him when he'd gone out, and the day of the wedding, he'd hidden anything of value in his apartment in one of his father's warehouses.

He made tea and tried to read a book about keeping proper—and improper—ledgers. Instead, he puzzled over the mystery of Matilda. She had expressed thanks but, even after all the notes, didn't trust him enough to give a hint about her plight. *The poor thing must be terrified*, said the shade of Nicky that visited him. As usual, that tiny remnant of his brother managed to make him uncomfortable.

Joshua considered finding Matilda and discovering why she was so afraid, but then he heard the voice of his family. *There's no gain to be made there, boy. Leave it be.*

He picked up the book about accounting and concentrated hard enough to drive off all voices.

A few days after Matilda left, Joshua visited his room in the warren, an old warehouse. He went late at night, when Matilda's family or Big Mervin's spies wouldn't be watching. He climbed up the rough brick wall, using the copper waterpipe to avoid the guard and other occupants. The familiar climb proved difficult with his damaged leg, but it felt good to move his body again. He sat on the windowsill of his room, admiring the ripple of the moon across the water, the rest of the darkness punctuated by a few moving boat lights and flickering lights on distant bridges. The gurgle and muddy reek of the Thames made him feel more alive than he had since the beating.

He eventually limped back to the marital apartment again, considering his future now that Matilda had scarpered. Her father didn't seem to notice her existence once he'd bargained her into Smith hands, but what if another member of her family or her friends wished to visit with her? There was also the matter of the nameless father of her child. Would Joshua divulge her address to any of them? No, he'd have to pretend not to know a thing about her strange, sudden disappearance. There, that should settle the imaginary remnant of Nicky lingering in his brain.

The secret of the vanished wife wouldn't last much longer. As Joshua opened the front door to the building of flats, a small man came out of the ground-floor apartment. Hardly a coincidence, Joshua knew.

"Evening," he said.

The man said nothing. He only scratched his red muttonchops and watched Joshua climb the stairs.

Big Mervin would keep police out of the matter, but they'd have suspicions about Joshua, of course. A Smith didn't shirk from violence, and his bride had been foisted on him.

Killing her and dumping her body into the Thames wouldn't be entirely out of the Smith character. He thought of his brother Nicky's murder. Once upon a time, Joshua had looked for Nick's killer, until his father had ordered him to stop.

A day after his father stopped him, Joshua discovered an obviously innocent man had been fingered for the crime. With that man out of the way, Big Mervin had gotten a nice new entry into a gambling business. Joshua had understood the truth of it. Big Mervin didn't care and perhaps had even ordered Nicky's death. Joshua didn't know and, after all this time, wasn't sure he wanted to find out.

He had his own secrets to hide now—or rather his wife's.

The next day, Joshua spotted the figure leaning in a doorway across from the building looking up at his window. Not one of Big Mervin's men, so it was likely one of her father's. Good. That meant *they* probably didn't know she'd gone, despite the red-haired man's snooping.

Joshua closed the rose-and-cherub-covered curtains, sad to block out the sunlight but unwilling to show anyone the truth until he had to.

Despite any possible difficulties her flight made for him, he admired her. A woman with a child on the way had been brave enough to run. Perhaps Joshua might try such a thing?

Running seemed...unrealistic. Big Mervin had tendrils all over London, and a still-useful son wouldn't be allowed to leave.

Joshua limped into the kitchen and made a cup of tea. His aching leg reminded him that he was now a flawed tool, so perhaps he could buy himself out at a reduced cost. Everything in the Smith family was for sale, and why couldn't he pay the price?

The harsh knocking at his door was too familiar.

Before he could open it, someone fumbled with a key. When the door swung open, McLeevy stood with a key in his hand, and next to him stood Big Mervin. "Josh, ha, you're here. But what about your wife?" His father pushed past Joshua. Two of his bully boys followed. "Where's your wife? Eh?"

Joshua closed the door and followed the small crowd into the hall. Big Mervin's amused questions showed he knew Matilda was absent, but he'd put on a show because he always did.

"Gone, is she? Take a look." His father waved a hand, and his boys, the Winter twins, walked around, opening doors, going into rooms, searching the apartment.

Big Mervin went into the drawing room and settled in a chair by the empty grate. "It's cold in here, boy. That won't do." He turned to one of the twins. "Set up a fire. Make a cup for me. We got some talking to do."

Joshua coughed and managed, "I got nothing to say."

"You can talk some better now. Yes, yes, still odd, but no, not bad, not bad. I thought you, your new condition, bah—a lost cause. But now I'm thinking you sound like the tomb itself. Voice'll strike fear into a body. That's handy. Better than doing the numbers even. And you have gained a bit of ferocity, I think." Big Mervin's smile helped him in the world: it turned his face into a map of curving, appealing lines that all shouted *I'm a jolly, trustworthy bloke.*

He waved a big finger at Joshua, who finally understood. Big Mervin was in a good mood because Joshua's wife wasn't there.

"I don't know where Matilda is," Joshua tried.

"Sure, sure." Big Mervin beamed at him. He laid his index finger on the side of his nose. *Our little secret.*

"I don't," Joshua said.

"You went out late at night, and we know you went to your rooms in the warehouse. What I like—" Big Mervin leaned close and tapped him on the knee. He kept his voice quiet. "What I really like is decisive action. Taking care of a problem."

Joshua stared at his grinning father, who practically burst with pride because his remaining son had taken care of a "problem."

Until two years ago, Joshua had worked hard to get Big Mervin's sunny grin aimed in his direction. His father's approval was a blessing, and there were strict rules about how he bestowed praise, gains and goals reached—mostly to do with pounds and shillings.

To get what he wanted, Mervin would sweep aside the weak, which had seemed reasonable to Joshua, until the weak was someone he cared about. When they found Nicky's body, Big Mervin had seemed pleased by the death—and Joshua understood the soul-deep ugliness of weeding out the weak.

After that, Joshua had made vague plans to slide away from the only home he knew or at least explore life outside it. The jaunt to that damned molly house for instance.

Big Mervin probably wouldn't come right out and say off a pregnant woman because she was a nuisance. The closest he'd come would be preaching about how the world belonged to the strong and ruthless.

Joshua stared at his father's face and realized he didn't want Big Mervin's glittering attention any longer. It was tempting to tell the truth, that his wife had run away. He'd admit he couldn't even keep track of a hugely pregnant lady, and then his father and the minions would march back out of the apartment in disgust. Joshua would be free.

He nearly did it, opened his mouth and said those words, until he realized if he did, someone would go after her. He'd seen her fear—her trembling hands that seemed to shake even when she'd written a note in Derbyshire.

Why had she been so bloody afraid?

Not your business. Tell him.

The girl'd had no one to count on other than some nameless friend. Not the father of her child and not her own father, who'd washed his hands of her.

His father was talking to him. "We'll use this place, why not? But you come on back to the rookerie—no, you come to the warren so we can talk about your new job, eh?" He rose to his feet and slapped Joshua on the shoulder. His vivid green eyes had just the right amount of humor and proud affection. Joshua felt a chill. He'd begun to climb up the organization again. He nodded.

"Say it," Big Mervin ordered.

"I'll be back. Soon."

"Yes, your new raven's croak sounds more'n sinister enough." He gave a laugh. "And probably best to slip out late at night again." The laugh died, and the eyes went hard. "But no more slipping off to that house of sodomy. It's a weak man who goes to those places. No more."

His worst insult, *weak*, linked to a threat. Joshua nodded.

"Say it," came the predictable order.

"I won't go to such a place again."

Big Mervin let his hostility show for another breath or two, then the smile broke through. "Your sworn word, and you know the penalty."

This time when Joshua nodded, there was no requirement for him to say anything. Big Mervin stretched his meaty arms over his head and walked to the door. He paused and summoned one of the twins.

"Make sure he comes around by tomorrow," he said to one of the Winter twins and jerked a thumb at Joshua.

"Do we hide the bride's disappearance?" The twin asked Big Mervin but watched Joshua with squinting brown eyes filled with a challenge. That meant Joshua couldn't allow his own gaze to drop.

Big Mervin pushed his tongue over a tooth and sucked noisily while he thought. "No reason to," he said after a long moment's consideration. "Her father is not strong enough to take us on direct. But he wouldn't, at any mark. He paid well enough to get rid of her. But no details necessary, mind. No questions answered."

He grew suddenly still, never a good sign, and eyed Joshua. "If she shows up alive and gone, it will make you look foolish. Don't want that to happen, eh? Worse, I'd look foolish, and that will *not* do. Understand?"

He sauntered out of the room, then he and his companions banged out of the apartment, though his presence had ruined the peace of the place.

Joshua went to the window and watched them go. Sure enough, another man emerged from the shadow of the alley and followed. One of Matilda's father's boys? The quiet road seemed filled with loitering men watching.

Recovery time and honeymoon were over, and he'd reenter the fold. The goal of his life had once been to be part of his father's crew, he reminded himself.

The only snag might come if his wife still lived and used his name.

Joshua tried to see himself ending her and couldn't. But helping her hide better—yes. And that would save them both.

Chapter Two

His grandfather's estate settled at last, Ross Munro sat in his grandfather's dusty house—no, *his* dusty house—and considered returning to Perth or perhaps even his own family's holdings in the Highlands.

The London funeral had been more than quiet, the only other mourners the old man's lawyer and housekeeper. Munro's late mother had always described her father as a nasty old curmudgeon, and Munro never had a chance to learn differently. Beyond formal letters exchanged at the start of every school term and Christmas, he'd had no relationship with the old man until Ross had arrived for the temporary London position. By then, his grandfather was so addled, he could barely speak.

Probably just as well the old man hadn't understood his only grandchild was a policeman.

And now that job had come to an end as well. Munro was at loose ends, still unclear where he belonged. He visited museums and attended lectures, usually about police work, because he couldn't shake his interest after a decade in the profession.

The housekeeper and cook were out when he slapped together bread and ham, sat in the vast kitchen, and made lists. Should he return to his old position in Perth?

He sighed and tapped the pencil on the paper. Would he stay in London? He had this house, but it would take a considerable effort to return to the police force here.

The Londoners he worked with had discovered his wealthy English family and public school background,, and the jeering began. "That how the haggis-gobbling Jock got the job over well-deserving Londoners?" a captain said in his hearing.

The cops who'd nearly beat that bruiser to death at Chester Street had already given Munro endless hell for stopping their fun.

He'd most definitely had enough. It had been an experiment for him to discover new ways of policing, and he cut it short. He couldn't regret the decision to leave the force.

He tore up his lists and fed them to the kitchen fire.

With the next day's post, a letter arrived offering a new opportunity. No need to try to work out a return to the force or to Perth. A come-down in his profession, but it would do for now.

He went to see his old school friend at the headquarters to say goodbye. Fairleigh had gotten him the position and was still sour that Munro would leave before the two-year position had ended.

They sat on either side of Fairleigh's desk in the new office built just for the investigators.

"You were only holding on until the old man died," Fairleigh grumbled.

"That is not why I'm leaving the force. I'm not at all certain I should even stay in the profession."

"Ha. You're a fine investigator. I don't see why you should give it all up. Is it still that incident in Perth?"

Munro figured the best way to cut off Fairleigh's interrogation was to be blandly polite. "I've learned a great deal during my months here in London, and I am much obliged for the experience."

"And now you're done policing in London as well. You don't do well with pressure, do you? You give up."

That seemed too close to the truth. For a long moment, Munro stared at the Union Jack fluttering outside Fairleigh's window.

"You are right. Henceforth I shan't," he said softly. It was something of a vow: he'd follow every case to a bitter end and abandon a job only when it became impossible to move forward.

After some more grumbling about ungrateful out-of-towners, Fairleigh admitted he'd heard rumors that life on the force had grown tough for Munro.

"That's not because you're not from London." Fairleigh rubbed his pale tobacco-stained mustache. "Turns out another reason the rank and file would hold a grudge against you. Rumor is that sodomite you saved a few months back was the son of Mervin Smith."

Chester Street again. And of course he hadn't heard that fact. No one at the station would share gossip with him. "And who's Mervin Smith?"

"A powerful devil. And that man you saved was one of only two surviving fruit of those poisoned loins. Apples and trees, from what I've heard."

At Munro's curious grunt, Fairleigh explained, "His death would likely have been a relief to all of London."

Fairleigh waved a hand. "Bad enough that we had a reprimand from on high, likely through one of Mervin's well-paid connections. The offspring of the devil won't even suffer from scandal of being a buggerer."

Munro folded his hands over his stomach, tried to keep his eyes steady and to change the subject. "He gave his name. I didn't believe him. I did learn he was released with the help of an expensive barrister."

"Hired by his father, no doubt." Alas, Fairleigh wasn't done talking about sodomy. "I expect Bloody Mervin couldn't care less that he's got a deviant son. Word is they've already quashed the rumor by buying junior a wife from another family of villains."

Munro wondered how he'd thought he could do the job without knowing the players in the game of London crime. Ah well, too late now. He did rather regret leaving the London job under a cloud, but he didn't care enough about the work to wait out the nasty look—not to mention worse nonsense like a dead rat left in his boots. "No need for them to grumble about me any longer."

"Your grandfather's money come through?"

"Some of it, yes, and I've got another job I think I'll take."

"Back home? This soon? So you are over it?" Fairleigh knew all about the case Munro botched in Perth—the main reason he'd fled to London. A young woman had died, Becky MacAllister gone forever, because Munro had to release a man he suspected was dangerous. Munro had scrupulously followed rules. Less than an hour later, the man had strangled Becky.

"Of course you are. You know there really wasn't anything to get over. It wasn't your fault." Fairleigh went on before Munro could answer, "I'll miss seeing your face around town."

"For now, I'm staying in London. I'm going to a private agency owned by an American named Kelly."

"Oh. Him." His friend sounded disgusted. "He asked me about you in a most roundabout way yesterday. He did ask about that very case. The Smith one. I had no notion it was a reference for a job. I would have said you were abominable at your work. It won't suit you at all, you know, to be peeking through windows at copulating couples to use in divorce cases. You like the rules and regulations, Munro."

He stiffened because, yes, he had liked to operate by the book in the past. And his strict adherence to regulations had been why Miss MacAllister had died.

Fairleigh was still jabbering on about Patrick Kelly. "He's as likely to skirt rules as any corrupt constable."

"We'll see." These days—too late for Becky MacAllister, but he hoped not too late for Joshua Smith.Munro had tried to loosen his tight hold to rules when he'd administered care in that jail cell.

After he left his friend, he went to meet his new employer, Patrick Kelly, at a restaurant not far from the Lambeth Bridge and the Royal Victoria Hall, called the Old Vic by the natives.

The grubby little place was filled with workers and only one person who had the rather too-good looks of an actor. And at that moment, that man stood up and waved Munro over. With his exuberant manner, blue eyes, and dark hair, Kelly could well have been a leading man on the stage. Too handsome for Munro's taste. He wasn't attracted to pretty people. If one was going to be a pervert, one might as well go in for all sorts of deviant tastes.

He did like Patrick Kelly, an exuberant American he'd met at a lecture given by a mutual friend about prison reform.

Munro had mentioned, without giving details, that he was on the lookout for a job. Apparently, he'd made a good enough impression that Kelly had offered one.

The American retook his seat at a table next to one of the two fireplaces in the casual restaurant. "Reminds me of the oyster houses down by the harbor in New York," Kelly said. "Long tables of drunk men sitting together, eating when they're not looking for a fight."

"You enjoy that sort of thing?"

"Bless you, no. I like remembering I don't have to go to break up fights in places like that anymore."

"You worked in a restaurant?"

"No, I was a cop like you, but for less time and I never climbed the ranks. Never got past walking the beat."

"In a far rougher city."

"Than Perth? Yes. And even than London, I'd say. New York is no picnic in the park. Life's too short for that sort of work."

"Mm," Munro agreed. "Yer a lang time deid."

"And for once you sound Scottish, instead of upper crust."

"The echo of my grandmother." He drank some beer. "When I get enough alcohol in me, I can't stop myself."

Kelly snorted and slapped the table. "Before you get maudlin, let's talk turkey. I have two cases for you. I'll let you choose your poison. One is to find a missing wife, and the other is to track the patterns of a straying wife. The second will pay better and be easier work."

"I'll take the missing one."

"Not so far removed from public service yet."

"Your meaning?"

"You'll go for the job that pays less but helps someone more."

Munro shrugged. That seemed about right.

Kelly finished his beer and gave a laugh.

"Hold on, let me tell you all first. The girl's father is our client, and he's as unsavory a character as you would ever care to meet. I'm hesitant about taking on the case because I think he'll never welcome police involvement, and in these matters, that's tricky. And you, still so fresh from the force yourself. It might be an advantage or a disadvantage. Danged if I can see which."

"Tell me the details, then. I expect I'll still take that case."

"Sounds straight out of romance, real Romeo and Juliet material, but I think our poor Juliet is a puppet. Two warring families, from what I can tell, both criminal concerns. Juliet is from the less successful family—her father's been convicted and done time. Not as smart or rich or patient as Romeo's pa, who's been charged more than once but not done more than a few hours in lockup. The two families who dislike each other have their own reasons for agreeing to this marriage."

The story of criminal families seemed to be popping up in Munro's life like snowdrops in spring. "Go on," he said.

"It could be the girl's father is worried about her."

"Could be? You don't sound convinced."

"With that crowd, it's all about money and power, you see. Money has changed hands, I don't know how much or what, and maybe just a dowry. I've heard a whisper that the bride had gotten herself into a situation and needed to find a husband fast."

"Ah."

"At any rate, young Juliet has vanished from her new marital nest, and her father believes it was not by her own free will. It could be a case of murder. And if it is, we'll contact the authorities, whether he likes it or not."

"Why would the groom agree to taking her on? The dowry?"

Kelly picked up a piece of cheese, stared at it, and put it down again. He pushed back his chair and scowled at Munro. "You were part of a raid last year, weren't you? On what my friend in the press called a 'more than usually transgressive brothel'?"

Munro nodded and tried to keep his face neutral. Kelly's close relationship with another man had created rumors strong enough to reach even Munro's uninterested ears. Mr. Sloan, the other man, was important and rich, and that meant two things: the talk of them was more interesting—and Sloan and Kelly had a nice layer of wealth to protect them from the gossip.

Munro said, "Yes, I was part of the raid. And I understand you were interested to learn I was. Shall I guess? The groom in this wedding was named Joshua Smith."

Kelly grinned. "Got it in one. What do you know about the Smith family? Or the Neely? The bride was Matilda Neely."

"Not much about the first, and nothing at all about the second."

"Neither did I until Neely came to me. He has a crew, I understand, but he didn't want to spread the word with his boys for some reason. I already knew that the older Smith—Big Mervin, he's called—is an eel who can wiggle out of predicaments that would put another man behind bars for years. Before his boy went to the wrong place at the wrong time and was idiot enough to attack a policeman, a Smith hadn't spent the night behind bars. And even Joshua has some of that Smith magic—he should have gotten at least two years with hard labor just for being a client of that place, and then add on how he got violent with the police."

"He paid a price." Munro thought about the battered body, near death, wheezing through a near-wrecked throat. The shattered leg, the foot twisted in the wrong direction. Munro swallowed, wishing that ugly picture would lose all power. "I don't expect he'll run easily again."

"Will he remember you from the raid?"

"I doubt it. He was still in and out of consciousness when his father's people took him away." Munro winced. "Others involved in the incident will never forget, though. I was not a popular fellow after I stopped the others from killing Smith."

"Aha. I imagine Mervin will know the story of your rescue of his son—he's good at gathering facts. I'll be glad to give the case to you, because those Smiths might actually be willing to talk to you. Want it?"

Munro nodded.

Kelly handed over a sheaf of papers. "Read these. Let me know if you have any questions. I'd go see the bridegroom, Smith Junior, first."

"Why not Neely?"

"He's uninterested in being interviewed often. Nervous Neely, I'd call him."

"Not even about his very own daughter?"

"That's what he said, and yes, seems mighty peculiar to me. But head over to Smith first. Not only is the apartment he currently occupies the last location where the bride was last spotted, but if he comes after you, you'll be able to run away. I hear Smith still has a limp."

Munro made a disgusted sound, but decided Kelly might be right.

After his new boss left, Munro sat and read through the information about Smith and Neely. There was virtually nothing about the missing woman.

He had a sense of urgency about this case, perhaps because of the ghost of his past, but also because, from what he could see, he was the only person set to hunt for Mrs. Joshua Smith. No action by the police, although considering her family, that made sense.

Matilda Neely Smith was only eighteen. How much knowledge of the world did she have? With much of the criminal class, age didn't mean much—some of the girls on the street were far younger than that, and they were hardly innocents.

He thought about Smith and realized the attack had taken place long enough ago, months now, he'd be healed as well as he could be. What did he recall of the man beyond blood, the ruined voice, that mutilated leg?

Smith had apologized. During one of his brief awakenings, he'd looked over at Munro and muttered *"I'm sorry"* several times. His bloodshot eyes might have been brown? Munro couldn't recall that, but he recalled the few words that came from him. Once, he looked at Munro and said, *"I should have tried harder. Nicky."*

He'd cried out when they'd set his leg, but there had been no cursing or screaming. Of course, with his injured larynx, screaming might have been impossible.

Smith's voice, cracked and rasping, was difficult to understand. His hair might have been any sort of brown, dark blond even. Hard to see under the filth and blood. Munro wasn't sure he'd recognize the man again. His features had seemed blunt, though that might have been due to his size.

Nicky, Nicholas. He flipped through and found the name in the papers from Kelly. One of Smith's sons, dragged out of the river.

Mervin Smith had sworn vengeance on the man he declared to be his son's killer, who just happened to be the man who owned the rookerie he wanted, a cluster around an alley near the docks. He'd set up the same sort of takeover before, Patrick Kelly had written. A death laid at someone else's feet, and Smith made a profit.

Could that have been what Joshua Smith meant when he'd said he should have tried harder?

In case Munro hadn't read between the lines on his own, one of the tiny footnotes read: *Police suspect Nicholas Smith's murderer to be one of Smith's own, but as usual, there is no proof or anyone willing to speak of the death.*

Munro carefully folded the four sheets of close script—the American's hand was sprawling, so someone else must have taken the notes. When he left the shabby but warm restaurant, he walked out into a gusting rain.

He pushed his hat down hard on his head and made a silent promise to the missing Mrs. Smith. A woman running in fear—he wouldn't skip any way to discover details. If she were alive, he'd find her and make sure she stayed safe. If she'd died, he wouldn't stop until he knew every element of truth.

The address for Mr. and Mrs. Joshua Smith lay in a quiet lane. His old guide book described the area of Clapham as low genteel: neither Grosvenor Square nor a Spitalfields hovel, and nothing like the territory Mervin Smith ruled.

The Smith apartment was up the stairs. The black-painted front door was unlocked, and Munro let himself into a house that had been clumsily transformed into several flats. He paused long enough to decide the ground floor seemed to be inhabited by large men with clumping feet.

Munro made his way up the broad staircase as quietly as possible, not wanting to draw the loud men into the hall—they might be associated with the Smiths or the Neely families.

He stopped outside the upstairs apartment to listen. They might have been footsteps, yes, and the steps seemed uneven, a hesitation as someone moved around. He heard another, louder thud. What was Smith doing? Dragging a body across the floor?

Munro tried the door—this one was locked. He raised his fist to pound, then remembered he no longer had the might of the law behind him. He'd have to behave as if he were a man alone and not a representative of an awesome force of justice. He stifled a sigh and gave a light rap.

The scraping and thumping stopped at once. He waited for the call of *who is it?* or something less polite, but there was only the rattle of the lock and the creak of the opening door.

Joshua Smith seemed too trusting for a villain.

The man who answered was taller than Munro expected and, judging from the loose way his clothes hung on his body, far less bulky than he'd once been.

His hair proved to be a dark brown, his eyes also brown— and filled with astonishment.

He must have been expecting someone else. Before Smith could slam the door, Munro put his foot in the opening.

"Afternoon sir," he said. "Mr. Smith, I expect?" He knew damned well it was Smith. He might have hollowed cheeks and his hair might be clean—not caked with filth and blood—but the man was identifiable. Those lips had been chapped to the point of cracking in prison, but they were recognizable: full with a distinct bow to the top lip, and there was a cleft in his chin as well.

Munro should not be staring at a man's mouth no matter how it would help him identify him. Time to seek out other identifiers. The Chester Street raid had left Smith with a gash on his right cheek from nose to temple, and yes, there was a trace of a white line under his eye.

Munro had spent a good deal of time examining the prisoner. But he argued with himself then that made sense since there weren't a lot of other things to look at in the prison cell when he was playing the part of physician for the man he'd thought was dying. And he told himself now that it helped him recognize his suspect. The man who might have killed his wife.

Smith stared back. He didn't attempt to slam the door.

"Mr. Smith," Munro said with more confidence now. "I don't require much of your time. I need to speak to you about a private matter."

Smith seemed to snap out of a fog. Perhaps he'd suffered brain damage? His dark eyes widened. "You're here." His voice was audible, but it carried the deep rasp that didn't fit a man in his mid-twenties or thereabouts, and the idea of addled seemed to fit his peculiar comment.

"Yes, so I am. Here to see you, in fact. My name is—"

"I know who you are," Smith interrupted. "Come in, then."

Chapter Three

Joshua had been expecting one or both Winter twins who were supposed to "help" him move, though everyone knew it was to drag him back into the family fold with no unwelcome interference from the Neely crew. Before his injuries, Joshua would have hated to be seen as in need of help and wouldn't have minded a bit of a run-in with the Neelys, but now he'd be glad for the twins.

Instead, he thought he had a stranger on his doorstep, but no. He knew this man.

Sergeant Munro was not as thin as he recalled, but since Joshua had lost so much weight himself, the whole world seemed fatter than his memory.

Joshua just gawped at the man, who looked odd in regular clothes and in a derby hat…and the sergeant stared back.

Joshua hurriedly looked away and invited the enemy in. He stared down at his feet as he backed away from the door. This man knew where'd he'd been the night he'd been beaten.

The few Smith blokes who knew what happened that night had been either amused or angry about Joshua's visit to the sodomites. They all had some response, and none were pretty.

Joshua stopped looking at men unless they stared, because he didn't want to get into any more "what are you looking at" arguments. He'd had at least one stare-down a day with the twins, but he couldn't allow himself to look away when dealing with them. He'd lose too much if he showed anything like deference.

And now with this sergeant, he let his eyes drop. For the first time with anyone other than Big Mervin, Joshua let himself duck and slink away, a coward's response, because he knew he owed Munro his life.

He hated Munro.

His guest apparently missed the whole toadying moment, because he was talking in a brisk manner with a tiny hint of the

accent that was exotic to Joshua, who'd never been outside of
London.

"Mr. Smith, what do you recall of our previous meetings?
Not much, I'll assume."

The brisk voice helped calm him. It had before, he
remembered now. Joshua looked up into hazel eyes. "You're
Munro."

"Yes, that's I. And you're Joshua Smith, caught in a
compromising position."

So much for the calm of that voice.

Joshua gaped at him, wondering what the hell he could want.
Blackmail wouldn't work. *Leave extortion to the experts*, he wanted
to tell him, but just waited.

"Just the sort of position a marriage might quash rumors
about."

The man's quirk of a smile and dry manner seemed to
contradict the menace of his words.

A threat rang out loud and clear. Should Joshua throw him
against a wall? The idea of putting his hands on that body was
actually appealing, but not for violence. Do not blush, he warned
himself. Do not think such things and then turn red.

His face went hot. He most definitely hated Munro.

"What do you want?" Joshua forced the words out louder
than usual, with less air, so that his voice was almost back to regular
again.

"Tell me what you've done with your wife."

Good to have the actual reason for this visit revealed at last,
but Joshua had to think, had to come up with an answer that
sounded real. He'd counted on his father and the crew not pressing
him for a real response or wishing him to say too much. He hadn't
bothered to come up with a believable explanation. Dull-witted
Joshua. He certainly wouldn't hand the truth to anyone.

He asked, "Who called the police about her?"

"No one. I'm not on the force any longer. I'm working for
myself."

The hint of a smile went away, and the way Munro's back went straighter—he must have realized what a silly thing that was to admit to a Smith. Yes, Munro damned well ought to worry about what would happen next.

Joshua's heart beat faster, but not with anticipation. He didn't want to toss Munro out a window or leer at him with threats or any of the standard business. He tilted his head to indicate the sitting room, then turned and stumped into it, trying not to let the limp show.

He slumped into a chair and waited for his guest to do the same before asking, "Why are you looking for my wife?" The words felt strange in his mouth. He'd hesitated too long between *my* and *wife*.

"Because she has vanished."

"Who told you that?"

"Are you saying she hasn't?" Munro folded his arms. "Then you won't mind if I settle down and wait to see her."

Joshua leaned forward, and the chair creaked under his weight. "She's none of your business."

"Let's not waste time. I've been hired to find her, Mr. Smith. And if you don't cooperate, I will go to the police."

The knock came that he'd been expecting. The twins.

One of them called out. "Oy. Time to go. You packed yet?"

Munro gave him a scowl. "Why are you leaving this apartment? I know Mr. Neely gave it to you and your wife. What's going on?"

This was the moment when Joshua teetered on a strange precipice. He could let the twins in. They'd meet, and Munro, if he had an ounce of brains, would say cheerio and be on his way. He'd hurry off, and that would be the end of it.

There was a chance Big Mervin wouldn't let such a thing stand, though, a former copper sniffing around their business. If Joshua let those boys in, that could spell the end of Munro. Might he convince the man to pretend to be on the police force still? Too much to explain, and his throat closed up as it did when he felt the rage or fear these days.

He put his finger to his lips.

Munro gave a single nod. He even got up and walked quietly to the kitchen, disappearing from the room as if he could read Joshua's mind.

Joshua took a moment to undo his collar before he walked to the door.

"Why'd you lock it?" the jeering twin asked.

"Habit. Come back in two hours. Three."

"What for? Let us in."

He remembered one of Peter Winter's peculiarities and played on it. "No, I'm…I'm sick."

One of the twins took a step back; the other rolled his eyes. That was one way to tell Peter from Bob. "You are red, come to think on it," Peter said.

"I'm sick," he said again. "A couple of hours should be fine."

Peter nodded. "Can do that. This place is yours after all. No urgent need to get you back to Big Mervin."

"Yes, he will understand." Bob stared at Joshua, then shuffled his feet and examined his own wrist, scratching at a sore. "But don't try to go home on your own. Got it? We'll get someone to watch over you."

"I'm a prisoner?" he couldn't help asking.

"Naw, guarded against circumstances. We've heard tell today that Neely is out on the hunt, looking for his daughter."

"He hasn't come here to visit."

Bob shrugged. "Word must have come back to him that she's vanished. Gossip, don't you know." The Smiths had spread the word to Neely, Joshua guessed. His father had been too delighted with the fact that Matilda was gone to keep it from the world.

"Just come back in two hours," Joshua said.

"You won't open the door to any of Neely's agents?"

He suspected it was too late for that. It did explain who'd hired Munro. Funny that he'd work for a man like Neely, who was near as bad as Big Mervin.

37

"Go," he growled.

"You're not up for guests anyway, are you," Bob said, mocking.

Joshua admitting he was under strength had made them a tittle more assertive than usual—he'd shown a new weakness on top of his old injuries.

He stifled a sigh and actually nodded to Bob.

It wasn't news that he'd end up needing to fight one or both to regain his place on the ladder. But it would be worth backing down at the moment to keep his visitor safe. The Winters would likely do to Munro what the police had done to Joshua.

The twins left, and he walked into the kitchen. Munro was hunting around and didn't stop when he entered. "What are you doing?" Joshua demanded.

Munro stopped opening cupboards and faced him. "There's only one cup and one plate next to the stove. She hasn't been here for days. Your wife is gone. You'd best tell me what's going on."

"You work for Neely. Why didn't you tell me that?"

"I work for a man named Kelly." Munro's gaze was steady, and he seemed entirely truthful.

Joshua took a step forward. "Oh? Then who is this Kelly to…to my wife?" He didn't mean to be loud, but he had better use of his voice than he'd been used to. He could speak more easily now. The days of silence must have helped heal him.

Munro held up both hands. His fingers were long and looked nimble. The hands of a lock picker. "Enough. Let us set this record straight. If you get violent, if I disappear, your troubles in that jail will look like a ruddy picnic compared to what will come down on you."

Joshua frowned. He could do threats as well as this man, though no, Big Mervin always said to toss in a reasonable tone with your pressure if you can.

"In that jail, you saved my life. I know." He nodded at the door. "Because of that, I owed you—and I just paid it off, keeping those blokes from you. I don't want to call them back but I will."

Munro's smile was broad and showed all his teeth.

"What's funny?"

"Ach, Mr. Smith, I watched you when you were recovering in jail."

Joshua held his breath. He didn't have a notion what this man was getting to.

"From what I witnessed, I came to understand you are not a violent man. You don't like to hurt people."

That was too much. Joshua held back his laughter that came out as a snort of astonishment. Apparently, Big Mervin wasn't his only visitor who liked to playact and cozen people.

Pointing out that he'd caught on to Munro's game wouldn't do, though he longed to. This sort of nonsense was when he missed Nick the most. He dasn't be silly with anyone else, as Nick said.

"I'm a lamb." Joshua jerked his thumb at his own chest.

Still smiling, Munro said, "If something has happened to your wife, I believe you weren't the one to do it."

Now that was a bold jump. Joshua expected Munro didn't mean a bit of it, but just in case, he nodded, trying to look earnest and believable. For a moment, Joshua even considered telling the truth.

Not on his life—or rather, not on his or Matilda's.

"It's no lie you don't work for Neely?" Joshua asked.

"I told you, I work for Mr. Kelly."

"Who's he?"

"He is worried about Matilda Smith," Munro said solemnly. "He cares about what has happened to her."

Kelly could be her unborn baby's father, then. It cheered Joshua to know someone cared for the girl, but he wasn't going to let a word slip until he knew for sure.

He'd kept the letter she'd sent and glanced toward it now. He'd write to her as soon as possible and ask about Kelly. If she gave permission, then he'd speak, but not before.

In the meantime, he'd keep the sergeant—ex-sergeant—out of his business and safe. Because if the fool poked around Smith business, cop or not, he'd be finished.

Joshua pointed at the door. "You best be on your way before my friends return."

"I can take care of myself."

Joshua shook his head. "No. You can't. You don't want to cross us. I know you're not so stupid to think otherwise."

"Aha, I was correct. You don't like violence."

Joshua managed not to roll his eyes. "Go away, Munro."

Chapter Four

Munro was stymied. In the past, he'd had success pouring on the butter. Something as simple as showing respect to suspects often loosened their tongues.

Usually, he spotted a sliver of humanity in even the worst people. He'd use that to slide into their confidence.

He had a knack for understanding traits or secrets people tried to keep hidden—a few words exchanged, and Munro could spot vulnerability or a delusion about themselves. He'd sensed Joshua Smith, a tough from the day of his birth, didn't like being a big nasty bully. The injured Smith on the prison floor had seemed capable of finer feelings—but perhaps he was simply an animal and Munro saw only what he'd hoped to see rather than God's truth.

Never mind, Munro wanted to find Mrs. Smith and would happily lie to find her.

Once upon a time, he'd been too fond of rules, and it had cost a woman her life. Never again. Finding her safe mattered more than Smith's true nature or Munro's honesty. If he worked hard enough to pretend being Smith's friend, he could get results even if the answer he got was directions to a shallow grave on Hampstead Heath. No, now he recalled that the notes from Kelly indicated the Smiths used the Thames as their personal bin for human waste.

"I think you want to help me," he said. "And if you did hurt her, you regret it. Then let me help you ease your conscience. I can help without consequences for you."

Smith's direct stare and smile that showed all his teeth with no humor in his eyes was designed to be unnerving. Such a strange response—and it could be a sign he was removed from humanity and took pride in violence.

Munro stood and pretended to be ready to go.

"Tell me what happened to Matilda, and I'll be on my way. Understand me, Mr. Smith, I only need to find the girl. I don't need to mete out punishment to anyone."

"No."

Munro hadn't pushed the honor angle hard enough. That might work. "You said it yourself. You owe me your life. Tell me details, and I'll consider all debts truly paid."

Smith's broad forehead wrinkled. Anger or simply concentration? He was a difficult man to read after all. Those eyes stayed steady.

"I have to wait," Smith said.

"For what? For your friends to come back?"

"No, no." He shook his head. "I'll meet you in four or five days."

"Why wait? Tell me now, and I'll get out of your life forever. I promise not to peach on you to the police or anyone else as long as I can find out what happened to Matilda Smith."

Smith made a disgusted sound. "It's not so easy."

That sounded promising, so Munro pushed a little.

"Tell me why not. Is it because your father is involved?"

A shadow crossed Smith's face, a moment of distaste or fear.

The single look seemed to hold the key, and Munro immediately tried it as a way to unlock his adversary. "Let me help you escape."

Smith absolutely laughed at that, a soft rasp that made Munro feel…trapped. He said, too belligerently, "I am entirely serious."

"Help me escape what?"

"Leave your father's…business, for lack of a better word."

Smith looked less amused. "You're a fool."

"I'm entirely serious. I can help."

"It's not all bad with him."

And that was an interesting response. Smith didn't say no to Munro's offer; he didn't say he wanted to stay.

"Oh? Do you think there are opportunities for a man such as I?"

Smith scowled at him as if he'd said something of dubious taste, but only said, "I doubt it. I can't help you in any way."

If Munro let him leave with his bags and those men, he likely wouldn't see Smith for days or perhaps weeks—and he didn't know if Mrs. Smith had that much time left, assuming she was alive.

Munro must flatter and seduce…no, when he recalled that night of the raid, not *seduce*. Not a word to use with a man like Smith, who apparently lusted after other men. The tight knot in Munro's gut squeezed and left him a little breathless and on the edge of queasy.

Remembering his goal of cozening Smith, he attempted a warm smile. When he thought about the man whose leg he'd set, the man who hadn't uttered a complaint, his smile felt more genuine. "If you help me, I will help you. Again."

Smith rubbed a hand over his face, seeming as weary and in pain as he'd been in the jail. "What do you want?"

"Tell me about Mrs. Smith."

"Meet me. Five days."

"Why must I wait?" Munro barked, then regretted his tone. Smith had said four days before and, if pushed, might make it six.

Once again, Smith's eyes moved, just a brief shift of direction—toward the window? No. He'd glanced at the table next to it. He said, "I don't have to explain myself to you."

Munro hadn't sat again, so now he walked about the room as if restless. When he passed the table, he looked down at a piece of paper and saw the words "talk to no one." But by then, Smith had pushed up from his chair. Before Munro could read more, Smith had limped over to the table, snatched up the paper, and jammed it into his pocket.

"What's that? Is it a ransom note?" Munro said. "Did someone contact you?"

Smith pointed at the door. "You're done here."

Munro stalked back to his chair and sat. "I'll go soon, but I have a couple of questions."

"Why should I bother with you?"

"Just a few questions. Don't forget, I have the power of the law behind me, Mr. Smith."

Smith limped closer. He wasn't bulky, but the menace of the man made Munro's heart beat too fast. Smith could smash a fist into Munro's face or haul him from the chair and toss him into the hall—after all, his arms hadn't been injured.

But he did nothing more than loom, a statue of a disapproving fighter ready to go to war. Not a drunkard, but an honest-to-God warrior watching and waiting for a signal to attack. Munro leaned away and then began to laugh.

"What's funny?"

"I threatened you, and now you're responding with a threat. It struck me as odd. This backing and forthing. It's like a dance."

Smith's genuine smile was a thing of beauty. The tension not only broke with that smile, light filled a dark room. "Most dances I know involve high-kicking women showing their drawers."

Munro gave a small gasp of annoyance when he recognized the powerful reaction coursing through him. This was unwanted and inconvenient.

Thank God, Smith didn't recognize the powerful bolt of attraction. "What are you looking at?" he said.

Munro shook his head.

Smith's cold look returned. His mouth thinned as if he'd caught himself unbending and didn't intend to do such a thing again. "Say what you will, then get out."

Munro breathed in and out several times, gathering himself together. He knew if he lifted his hands, they might be shaking with fear—and need. Best not look at the body standing before him. He plastered a smile on his face and gazed at something over Smith's shoulder. His powerful, muscular left shoulder.

Aim for the prize, Munro reminded himself. Back to business.

Their moment of shared amusement had been promising. He needed Smith as an ally and would work toward that. Form a bond first, because threats would only make the man close down fast again.

Munro launched into his song and dance. "Calm yourself, just a few questions, to get to know each other, ye ken. A bit of a chin-wag, nothing so bad. The sort you might have with the lads in a pub." He tilted his head to the side, tapped his temple with his finger as if to jog his mind along. He hoped he looked comical or harmless like any tipsy good-natured fellow. "Tell me this. If you could go anywhere, do anything, what would it be?"

Smith didn't answer. He didn't so much as twitch.

Munro cast about wildly to come up with his own answer. Or rather the right answers to draw out responses from Smith. "What I'd do, what I'd want to do is, ah, go back to Scotland. That's where I'm from. I'd maybe…"

He paused as he tried to think what the devil he could say. Not *be a copper,* that wouldn't work with Smith, who surely was brought up to hate the police, and never mind the Chester Street beating. Nor would the pretense of longing to be a solicitor be the right thing to say. What would seem exotic to a London dweller?

Munro thickened his accent. "I'd raise sheep and so on. Och, there are these coo with horns you'd ne'er believe." He raised his hands and outlined exaggerated imaginary horns on either side of his head. "Giant shaggy beasties called Highland cattle."

He had no interest at all in animal husbandry, but the man's stare was getting to him, and he havered on about the countryside and cows.

Smith didn't move. No, that wasn't true—his cheek twitched as those dark eyes stared into Munro's face.

At last he looked away, releasing the terrible pressure created by that gaze. In his hoarse voice, he whispered, "You're mocking me."

"What the divil kin ye mean? I'm sakeless." He'd gotten his father and grandmother's accent and words stuck in his mouth. Munro tried again. "I mean to say, I'm not mocking anyone."

"Who've you been talking to? Who?"

"About what topic? My ambitions for life?" Munro had apparently lured his fish, but wasn't sure what sort of fight he'd taken on.

"About..." Smith took a step back, his bad leg banging into a small table, but he didn't appear to notice. He held up a hand to either steady himself or stop Munro's words. "Never mind."

Munro smiled and went on. "Because I've never said a word to anyone about how I long to move to the country and raise animals." That was the God's honest truth, because he'd never held such a desire.

"No, about me."

Munro understood at last. "You? That's what you want, you mean?"

Smith gave a single nod, then appeared to regret it. "Never mind," he said again.

Munro rose to his feet again, an idea of how to keep Smith interested popping into his head at last. But he wanted to be able to run away if he'd gotten it wrong and Smith took offense. "Your desire..." No, bad idea. They both knew what Smith's desires had tangled him up. "What you want from your life is to go to the country. Perhaps to have animals as well?"

Munro wanted to say more, but clamped down on that urge. Silence coaxes words out of the suspect, as Fairleigh used to say. *You're the only Scot I've met who can't get the point of quiet.*

He waited and passed the time by staring at Smith. After all, that glaring method had worked on other people, although this proved the first time he was as unnerved as any of his subjects. He'd force himself to ignore the disturbance storming in his own body.

Smith rubbed a hand over his forehead, pushing at his hair, which fell into his eyes. He needed a cut, though the longer hair suited him. He appeared older than Munro had first thought in jail. Even when he'd been passed out on the stone floor, face drawn with pain, Smith had seemed just out of boyhood. It had been his pink cheeks and that mouth. Although from what he'd read about the Smiths, perhaps more than his appearance gave him the look of an unfinished man. All those years as a dogsbody for his father, who didn't allow his underlings to say "boo" to a goose without permission—no wonder Smith hadn't grown up.

Now he looked weary and closer to thirty years of age than twenty. "I did want that once," he said at last.

"To escape this city?" Munro asked, as gently as he could, considering how much he ached to drag out his watch and check the time. He should have felt more in control of the conversation, not to mention pangs of unwelcome desire.

And he had more than his own weakness to consider. How much longer did he have to work on Smith before the others returned? He didn't dare look impatient or indifferent, however.

"Did you tell anyone you want to leave London?"

Smith nodded. "I admitted it to one person. He's gone three years now."

Munro recalled Kelly's notes and dates. "Your brother, Nick."

The way Smith recoiled—those words had been a mistake. But no, because now Smith only looked uncertain, not closed up or angry. "How did you know?"

"I didn't. I hazarded a guess," he lied. "You used his name and seemed to talk to him when you were feverish in jail. He was your friend?"

Smith rubbed his head again. The man appeared close to tears. Was it guilt from killing his brother or from the loss? Either way, he didn't answer. He drew in a couple of long breaths, then let his hand drop to his side. "This has nothing to do with you. Or my...wife." Again, the pause between *my* and *wife*. He either wasn't used to the word "wife"—or he hated saying it. Munro would give ten guineas to discover which.

He tried, "Does Mrs. Smith like the country?"

Smith's hand brushed his pocket. The one with the letter in it. It could mean nothing, Munro reminded himself as he said, "Is that where she is? Did you send her to the country?" Please, God, let that be the answer.

"I sent her nowhere. You're done here."

"Sorry, sorry, I wasn't going to mention her." He raised his hands in a gesture of surrender. "We'll talk about you instead and—"

47

"No."

He rolled on, trying for the pleasant voice, but louder. "Because I have a fine idea. I can help you. Remember I said so. And you want to escape London, yes?"

"I never said that. What the hell are you talking about? If you can't find your way out of here, Munro, I don't mind showing you how. Get your arse—"

"Here's what I can do for you. I can help you do both, hide and go to the country. Help you escape to the country. I have a place. No one goes there. No one would find you there. There's only a wee village nearby. And the mists and mountains and the loch…" He went on about the god-awful empty place as if it were heaven. His other grandfather had left him the damp falling-down pile of stones, and he hadn't been there for nearly a decade. He'd said quite a bit about the views of grasslands, his imagination gone nearly wild as the land itself. Smith had stopped interrupting and listened intently.

Munro had no intention of helping this villain, only of doing his job. But when he allowed himself the moment to look at Smith, really look at him, there was an expression of something close to hope in those eyes.

Munro shifted his gaze away, but it was too late. He'd already noticed too much; for instance, that Smith's eyes were the color of teak, and they were filled with a vivid longing.

He walked to the door, disgusted with himself and ready to move on to the next interview subject. He'd visit Neely, the man who'd actually hired him. Should have started there, he supposed.

Just before he left, he turned back to Smith, who stood with his hands buried in his trouser pockets. One more attempt. "I will help you leave the city on the condition that you tell me that your wife is safe."

Smith laughed, a soft puff of air. "If I wanted to leave, I would've." He licked his lips, and that knot in Munro's gut twisted hard. "But all right. Tell Kelly she's safe."

Munro believed him. His shoulders ached, and he realized he'd held them tense from the moment he'd walked into the apartment. The last four words let him release those muscles.

"Good. That's very good. Where shall we meet in a few days?" He expected he'd find the girl by then, but best to play along with him in case he needed Smith again.

"The Lamb and Flag in Covent Garden."

"Good. That's neither my territory nor yours."

"Territory." Smith nodded. "Good word for it, eh?"

"Half two, in four days, I shall see you there," Munro said.

He turned to leave, and then Smith changed his plans again by glancing out the window and commenting, "There are watchers. Go out the back."

"Why?" Munro demanded. "Didn't your friends say they'd be back? Are they hanging about?"

Smith shrugged. "The watchers are probably Neely's men. They've been here for days."

That was annoying and a reason to go to Neely's house. Someone had to be in charge of this case, and not just sending separate parties of men to track down Mrs. Smith.

Had Neely's men already questioned Smith? He'd have to find out. He was here already and decided not to leave immediately after all. He squeezed his hands into fists and let them go to release the tingle from unspent desire and tried to force himself back to thinking about his work.

Chapter Five

Munro had that calculating look, so Joshua knew he was about to try something again. The policeman had startled Joshua badly with that comment about longing for the country. Could someone have overheard his words to Nicky a few years back as they'd downed a couple of pints together in a pub? Did Joshua really moan about it when he was in the jail? Likely time in the country was the cop's honest desire or some sort of lucky guess. It couldn't be actually knowing Joshua at all. Still, it felt a tad revolting having that old desire dug up—as if a grave had been invaded. Hearing that private longing said aloud in that rich voice gave him a turn. Blimey, that accent he donned and took off easily, like some kind of polished top hat.

Now Munro said, "If the lads outside are Neely's men watching you, they've probably heard rumors and are worried about their employer's daughter. I should go talk to them."

Joshua gave another laugh. His throat had grown used to the sensation again, and it did not hurt or startle him this time. "You best hope you hear from me in four days and not any of the Neelys."

"What does that mean? They have no reason to come at me with their fists."

Joshua had been talking of Matilda's safety, not Munro's, but didn't bother correcting him. "I don't trust my father-in-law, not that I've met the gammy cove."

"The what sort of cove? No, no, never mind. Why do you distrust him? What's wrong with Mr. Neely?"

He seemed genuinely interested, and once again, Joshua decided he might tell the truth, as long as he didn't give hints about Matilda's location. "I think she's afraid of him."

"Mrs. Smith?"

"Who else?"

"Afraid of her own father? Why do you think that? Did she tell you in so many words?" Munro sounded troubled.

"More an impression, and that's all I'll say." He paused. "All I can say, seeing as how I don't know much at all."

"If you're not lying—" Munro broke off. His eyes widened. For the first time, he looked astonished. "Ah, that's so? I think you're not protecting yourself with this four-day wait for information. You're protecting her."

"More like I'm busy."

"I'd believe that excuse if we hadn't talked for far longer than it took for you to say the simple words to me. Come now, you could just say them." He let his speech drop and go quiet, a bad imitation of Joshua's ruined voice. "Mrs. Smith is away or Mrs. Smith is hiding or I've put Mrs. Smith's body in the back bedroom."

That last made Joshua laugh. He could almost hear Nick's comment: *you always did have a sad notion of what was funny.* Or maybe it was just this Munro with his dry comments. He'd had such cold eyes in that prison even as he'd come to Joshua's aid. He'd seemed a man of few words but had prattled today. He'd been dignified and brisk before, and now he imitated the happy drunk in a local pub.

Ex-policeman Munro intrigued Joshua.

That explained why Joshua had let him stay on and hadn't simply opened the front door—or a window for that matter—and dumped the man out. He'd paid his debt by protecting Munro from the Winters. He owed him nothing more.

Best to admit the irritating truth to himself: loneliness played a part in letting Munro hang about. "Aren't you leaving now?"

"I don't know how to get out the back of this place," Munro said. "You'd better guide me."

This seemed like another of Munro's strange ploys, but Joshua couldn't think of any harm in showing the way.

They couldn't go down the narrow servants' staircase side by side. Joshua motioned for Munro to go first. He wasn't about to let a stranger go behind and see how much it hurt him to take the steps—or to give Joshua a hearty shove from the back and watch him take a tumble, though that seemed the sort of jinkery the Winters would get up to if they wanted him out of the way. Munro

51

could simply call one of his friends on the police force to take care of the problem of Joshua.

And why had he left the police? Joshua wanted to ask but supposed the man wouldn't answer, especially not in the corridor where his words would be overheard.

When the house had been divided into apartments, the servants' entrance was moved to a side door, out of the kitchen. It opened onto a narrow corridor and a stone wall with a gate out to the back. Joshua suddenly recalled that the wrought iron gate squealed like the very devil, and if someone was keeping close watch on the house, they'd probably hear that squealing gate half a block away. As Munro reached for it, Joshua grabbed his arm.

The ex-policeman seemed to explode. There was a sudden whirl of his whole body and a slam of his arm. Joshua ended up on the slate path, facedown, the wind knocked out of him with a wicked elbow blow to the belly.

When Joshua could breathe again, he rolled onto his back and looked up into Munro's eyes. There was the grim, cold expression—the man's true nature plain on his face again, all pretense of good nature gone. Joshua knew plenty of his type, a man who wouldn't let finer feelings get in the way of his goals and the thin coat of friendliness ripped away at the first threat. This basher version of Munro was more believable than the one who'd offered some peculiar sanctuary.

Joshua whispered, "I was trying to stop you opening the gate at the back. It's loud. Squeaks."

"Oh no! I beg your pardon." Munro slid the good-natured mask on easily.

Joshua ignored his reaching hand and hauled himself up, wishing he could still jump to his feet. Now he had to climb carefully like an old man. Bloody cops.

"I thought you were attacking me," Munro also whispered. "I acted on instinct to protect myself."

"From the cripple?" Joshua laughed. Again. Why Munro amused him was beyond his understanding, especially at the moment with his arm in pain and his stupid leg aching as well.

"From the report I've read and what I witnessed that night, you're well able to protect yourself, at least one on one." Munro's smile didn't reach his eyes. He peered about the small back garden.

The noise of the brief—and embarrassing for Joshua—bout might have disturbed someone. Munro also seemed in a hurry to be off.

"I believe you about the gate. I'll climb over the wall," he said. And with that, he jumped and grabbed the top of the stone wall at least a half foot above his reach. He hauled himself up to straddle the wall on his stomach, moving as quickly as if he were in a race.

"Four days, the Lamb and the Flag," he told Joshua before dropping, with only a slight rustle and thump, to the other side, into the neighbor's garden.

Joshua made his way back up the stairs. He snooped through his marital apartment one last time, looking for goods, looking for answers to where his wife had gone and why.

Someone shouted something outside—a cry of happiness—a costermonger, likely.

When the Winter twins showed up an hour later, they came with their grinning older brother.

Right away, Joshua knew something was off. Egbert "Cold" Winter was one of Big Mervin's favorites and only left the rookerie and lanes in his charge under orders from the big man himself.

Best way for Joshua to hide his fear and dislike of this Winter brother was to act as if they were good friends. "Hullo, Cold. Nice of you to come, but no need for your help."

"Ah, but there is!" Cold's laugh was genial. "I'm here to do inventory so we can sell it all for you. Got a nice fence to do the job. And we're here for the other reasons too."

All three brothers wore unnaturally wide smiles, and the hair on Joshua's neck rose.

Cold nodded to Peter and Bob. "You two start. Go on. Another room."

They scampered away. Few disobeyed Cold Winter, not even his brothers.

"Big Mervin didn't say a word to me about selling this stuff. My stuff," Joshua said.

"Didn't he?" Cold made himself at home on a pink sofa, tossing the tassled pillows on the floor and resting his feet on them. "Well, just as I 'spect you don't know much at all, like he's found you'd broken your word."

"What?"

"We'd wondered why you got special treatment in jail. We heard from one of our singers who'd been dragged in just that day."

Singer. An informant. "Who's we?" Joshua asked. "You and your brothers the jackals?"

Cold ignored the question. "You got done down hard, but you survived. And then we hear it's because you got a special little angel helping you out. Did he know who your father is, we asked ourselves? Not likely, we decided, since he's not from around here. He must have had his own reasons, and judging from the sort of brothel where you were nabbed, we can guess what it was." Cold stopped to shudder. "Disgusting. Never would have thought it of one of Big Mervin's own sons."

"What the hell are you getting at?"

"All about your special friend, the rozzer who paid a call on you today. Yeah, we know why you sent off the twins a couple of hours ago. Feeling unwell indeed. Likely your arse hurt from being buggered, eh?"

Joshua couldn't let that one stand, not if he wanted to survive. And words wouldn't fix it—no need to bother with them, then.

He no longer moved quickly, so he'd be broadcasting his intentions. That meant Cold had time enough to come up off the sofa for the attack, and Joshua planned for that. Just before they smashed together, he ducked down and drove his shoulder into Winter's middle. That went well enough, but, without warning, Joshua's leg gave way, and Cold landed on top of him.

"Get off me!" Cold screamed. Real fear was in his voice—there'd be some history there that Joshua didn't know about. And didn't care neither. He had to finish this.

He didn't have much room to draw back his fist, but he managed to put some momentum into his next blow, right into Cold's face.

With a loud curse, Winter jackknifed to the side and off Joshua. He rose to his feet, still stumbling when he hit one of the many tables and crashed to the ground.

When the twins came barging in, they saw Winter sprawled on the floor and Joshua pulling himself up.

"Need us?" Peter asked Cold, and glared at Joshua.

Cold rubbed his bloody nose on his sleeve. "Get out, Peter."

"They're staying." Joshua took charge—it was his right as the fight's winner. "And one of you is going to tell me what happened to Munro."

"That's the cove we found sneaking about?" The twins didn't smirk or sneer. That meant Big Mervin wanted the news of Joshua's sins and the identity of the rescuer kept secret from the foot soldiers. Cold knew the details, but these boys didn't.

"Sergeant Munro," Joshua said. "A cop, and you know it. He was here on an investigation."

"Investigation, is that what you call it?" Cold spat blood onto the floor and wiped his hand across his mouth. "Don't lie to us. He's not on the police any longer, Joshy."

"Yes. He. Is. Still a cop." Joshua carefully slowed his words. Nick had told him he spoke in a rush when he was blurting out lies, and maybe Cold had figured that out too. "He works for a special…section of the force." That sounded real, he hoped.

He pointed at Cold, astonished that his finger didn't shake. "You haven't killed a lawman, have you? That would be a big mistake. Big Mervin doesn't like the sort of attention it'd bring. I'm asking again. What happened to Munro?"

"He's in the coal cellar. Back in our digs. Trussed and muzzled and batty-fanged a bit," Peter said. He might bow down to his brother Cold, but he still knew better than to cross the boss's son who'd just won a hand-to-hand. "You didn't say nothing about a cop, Cold."

"He's battered pretty bad," Bob added. "If he's a cop, well then, I guess the only choice we got is to finish. River's right there and waiting."

"No, that's not on. I got something I need to get from him. Information. I got to find out about some plans from him." Joshua rushed now.

"Plans for what?" Cold wiped blood from his upper lip, hiding his sneer of disbelief.

Joshua was going too fast and hot to let him interrupt. "If you idiots kill him, we'll get all sorts of trouble. About what you've done to him. If he's alive still, then…" He swallowed hard, tried to slow his words and to keep any quavers from his voice. "We can pay him off."

"What? A cop? They're expensive. 'Specially a sergeant," Peter said.

"No. It won't take much. In fact, I can do it. I have savings." Damn it, he had to slow down. He sucked in some air, careful and silent to ease the panic. His throat hurt. He hadn't spoken this much in months.

His pause gave Cold a chance to speak. "You care too much," Cold said. He glanced at his brothers but didn't say anything else.

Yeah, he kept quiet about the Chester Street event, likely under orders from Big Mervin. That regretful glance in their direction said there was nothing more Cold wanted to do than announce Joshua's sins to his brothers.

Joshua knew the best way to stymie that sort of babbling. Turn the light around and shine it on Cold.

"I have a business arrangement with Munro, you pervert. What kind of nonsense are you talking about? *'Caring'*? I got to get information. You ruin that, and you ruin more than you know."

"I didn't hear nothing about that from Big Mervin." Cold sounded sulky now. "Not what he told me." More blood trickled down from his nose but he didn't seem to notice, not even when it dripped onto the floor.

"We get back there, and I'll get what I need from the cop," Joshua said. "We'll go, now."

Bob hitched up his trousers. "First we fill the wagon. Right up to the top. We want to do it in daylight so any Neely hanging about might see. It sends a message, understand."

Peter added, "Yeah. This is a Smith flat, and we do with the insides what we want."

"This is *my* place," Joshua said. "But I'll say you can come and go any time. You load the wagon if you want. I'm going."

He walked to the door hoping to hell the pain in his leg didn't make his limp worse than usual. Without looking back, he left the building. If the Winters didn't come along soon, he'd have to walk a bit to find a hack, but that was likely best. Then he could go find Munro and get him out without the Winters interfering. The lady everyone called Mother Winter, their mother—or maybe she was an aunt or granny—ran the house on the dead-end alley where the Winters were squatting at the moment. She and her boys might run the whole blind maze of that rookerie, but she was hardly going to stop a Smith from going into the coal cellar...or so Joshua hoped.

Cold ran after him and caught up too easily. "The boys will load the wagon. You and I can go talk to this Munro."

Joshua didn't bother answering. He'd have to walk without wincing and try not to limp any more than usual.

"What are we going to get from him?" Cold was obviously still suspicious as hell, which wasn't ideal, but Joshua hardly cared.

"That's my business."

"Should be about the family, not you."

"Did I say otherwise?" They had to stop to let a wagonload of barrels pass. "You're not my keeper, Cold."

"Much you know."

"Clever retort, chuckaboo." He knew Cold hated mockery. "But I'll get my marching orders right from Big Mervin, not a cow-slavving imitation of my pa."

He made sure Cold walked in front of him until they found a hack.

Mother Winter either was out of the house or she was hiding. Joshua was just as glad not to cross paths with the skinny woman. She seemed a ghost, with blurry blue eyes that stared at anyone who came through the door, and as she stared, she'd run her hand up and down the bundle of rags at her side—the bundle that contained a rusty knife. Peter once told Joshua they'd offered to give her a good leather holster, but she liked her rag holder better. *"Old twaddlewit seems to think it's hidden there. As if no one knows."*

Cold led Joshua to the back of the house. He unbolted the door, and they climbed down steep wooden steps to a cellar that smelled of coal and rats. The only light came from two half windows near the coal chute. Joshua, who had good eyes for the dark, could see that one of the piles on the floor was shaped like a man sitting up.

Joshua stood behind Cold and mimed sleep, putting his finger to his lips and closing his eyes for several long seconds. If Munro was dead or passed out, the idiot act was useless.

If he could see well enough and understood Joshua mumming, then it might save his life. And if he struggled to show he was alive? Joshua briefly considered fighting Winter or anyone else in the house or in the whole of the rookerie to get Munro out alive. He realized he might be willing to step in this time, not so much out of fondness for the ex-policeman, or even out of the debt he still felt he owed. *You failed before.* He usually dismissed the thought easily, but now it came along with a new one: *Don't fail this time.*

Chapter Six

Munro's side hurt so much, he suspected the goons had probably cracked or broken a rib. He hadn't passed out, which was a pity. Unconscious would be preferable to lying and then sitting in a cellar, waiting to die. His hands had been tied, but in the front, a small blessing. His feet had been bound, but he couldn't reach the knot. Even without the rope around him, the windows in the room were too small to wiggle out of, and the door at the top of the stairs too sturdy.

His nose hurt from a blow or two, but he had to breathe through it, very carefully, since his mouth was out of commission. In fact, the corners of his mouth felt as if they'd been sawed into bloody wounds by the cloth that gagged him.

Years ago, Munro had gagged an angry prisoner who'd been screaming obscenities at everyone entering the jail. If he survived this event, Munro would go find that man and apologize, though, no, the fellow had likely ended up dead in a ditch somewhere, killed by someone he'd insulted. Probably where Munro would end up as well.

He heard the sound of the door slamming shut over his head, so he stopped exploring his prison and hopped back to the place they'd dumped him after the beating.

Less than a minute later, two large men came clumping down. One was the nasty bit of work who'd hit him. He'd forced Munro to talk, and he'd stuck to a version of the truth. Always did seem best to stay with something like facts that wouldn't hurt anyone.

The other man proved to be Smith—thank the Lord. Although why did he think that was a good thing?

Munro was about to indignantly demand to be released when he noticed Smith lolled his head to the side and mimed sleep.

Fine. But if they beat him again, he'd fight back again. He closed his eyes, tried to concentrate on breathing slow and easy.

"Did you kill him?" Smith walked over and dropped to a crouch next to Munro. His large hand rested on Munro's neck. Choking? No. Munro considered twisting away from the warmth, then smashing his bound feet up at Smith. And then he realized the man was taking his pulse or pretending to.

"Christ, his heart's faint, barely going. Too slow."

No it wasn't. Munro could feel the thumping in his throat, strong and regular, though a bit faster than usual.

Smith straightened and rose to his feet with some difficulty. "Cold, you and the boys are good at smashing, but you're not masterminds if this is your idea of a clever plan."

"Big Mervin wanted the man grabbed and questioned," Cold reminded him. "So he vanishes after, why not? He's not important."

"Oh-ho! I got it now. What of it indeed. Aren't you clever." Smith's voice was a frightening low rumble. "You knew Munro would have to report to his station just exactly where he'd go today. My apartment. The cops would know he was visiting me. You knew they'd send someone after him, and hey presto, the police would be after me. You're trying to get me killed or locked up."

Interesting. A person's first impression of Smith might be of a gormless limping bully, but he had some brains, throwing accusations at Cold. Or maybe he believed that load of manure he'd just slung, that Munro really was still a cop.

"Christ, no. I just saw him sneaking about next door to your apartment, took him for a lone Neely man who'll talk."

"So you say now." Smith growled again. "But you told me he was a rozzer, so you knew. You made my life a difficulty and, maybe worse, stopped me from finding out what I need to know."

"What is that, eh? Why should I—"

"It's to do with my wife. Now you see why it's Smith business, but none of yours."

Something shoved at Munro, just missing the sharp pain in his side. He slitted his eyes open enough to see that Smith had nudged him with a boot.

"He's still alive, for now. Cold, you go on upstairs, check outside. Make sure no one's about to see. I'll bring him up, and don't you get in my way."

"I'll tell Big Mervin."

"Don't sell me a dog, Cold. I know better. You just tell him how you beat up a bluebottle for no good reason and see where it gets you."

"He'll see why we did it. He won't see what you're up to."

"You know better than to go messing with the law. Like Marsh after he gutted the copper. You remember?"

"That's not anything like—"

"Marsh didn't wait for the right moment. Blood all over the street in daylight. Remember what Big Mervin said? Being smart is better than being right. And what else did he say?"

"Jesus, I'll take this from him, but not the likes of you."

"He told Marsh—the now dead Marsh, mind you—that when you grab your cock and wave it around, make sure you're in private. Keep it hidden in your pants unless you got some deal that'll be made stronger with the showing of it."

"Just about right, you remembering a story with cock in it."

"Shut it, Cold. You owe me for hiding your mistake. Just shut your gob and go. Keep them eyes peeled for trouble."

Cold went up the stairs.

Smith stood absolutely still as the door closed behind Cold.

"He didn't shoot the bolt," Smith muttered. "Maybe I'll get out of here alive."

Of course, these criminals would murder each other over anything.

Smith leaned over and loosened Munro's gag. As Munro gasped and clumsily rubbed at his lips with his tied hands, something scrabbled close by in the dark.

"Holy Christ," Smith croaked. He jumped back, stumbling a little.

"A rat," Munro said. They'd started to come out, probably drawn by the smell of his blood. "They're frequent visitors down here."

61

"You, shut it. Be knocked out good and proper till I say otherwise."

Munro considered protesting but decided to heed Big Mervin's advice to keep private. He'd stay hidden and not wave anything around.

"Right. Get up," Joshua whispered. "I got to haul you like a sack, but not until we're up the stairs." He rubbed his thigh about where Munro recalled the femur had broken a few months earlier.

"No interest in falling on your arse again today?"

The strange chuffing in Smith's throat might have been laughter.

Munro managed to push himself to his feet. The rope binding his ankles had loosened during his flailing around the cellar room, but now he teetered and nearly fell over.

Smith waited by the bottom of the stairs, watching. As Munro rocked, Smith gave an impatient grunt, walked over, and wrapped a solid arm around Munro's shoulders. They lurched and hopped to the stairs.

They were probably a comical sight, but Munro was grateful for the warmth coming off the large body keeping him upright.

The gratitude died when Smith held up the gag. Munro shrank away, embarrassed to hear a faint whine come from his own mouth.

Smith leaned close. Instead of telling Munro to stop sniveling or insulting him, Smith only breathed a few words in his ear. "I won't tie it tight. Just until we get away from the alley."

Munro nodded, and the gag was back, chafing the tender corners of his mouth again. They made their way carefully up the stairs, Munro moving up step by step on his arse, ahead of Smith. At the top, he turned to face Smith so he could half fall, half be hauled up onto his big shoulder. The pain was enough to make him gasp. He should have said something about his rib before the gag went back in his mouth. He wiggled frantically, trying to shift position so he didn't feel as if a knife had been lodged in his body.

For several moments, in horrific discomfort and his head upside down over Smith's back, he was sure he'd be sick. But with another grunt and a shove. Smith arranged him so that he somehow rested on both of Smith's shoulders, as if he were some kind of human yoke or a tied calf. The sharp stabbing pain lessened, and Munro decided the bone was intact. He'd once fallen off a horse and broken three ribs. A slight change of position wouldn't have affected that agony.

Smith's arm looped between Munro's legs, under his knee, and he grasped one of his arms, though both dangled down his front since they were tied. Munro closed his eyes and tried to imagine how he'd escape this mortifying hold.

Trussed like a helpless animal.

The jostling of Smith opening a door and sudden draft of outside air distracted him from his current misery.

"Nobody about?" Smith said.

Cold's voice answered. "Where're you headed? Back to your warren?"

"Don't think so."

"Where?" Cold's voice came from nearby. He stood not far from Munro's head.

"I'll get word to Big Mervin."

"Find a way to snuff Munro's candle." Cold—that name suited the man who had ice in place of any warmth or finer feelings. "He saw me and the boys. Best for you too, and you know it."

"Maybe."

The single word made Munro flinch just a little. Smith hitched him up a bit and took a firmer grip on his wrist. Thank goodness Smith seemed uncommonly strong, or Munro would worry about being dropped.

"Here's an idea, Cold. You go on back to my apartment and load up the wagon with the boys. Make it loud, drop the pianoforte out a window, why don't you? And maybe stop in for a pint. Draw enough attention to yourselves, and you'll have witnesses aplenty for the time this one"—he gave a shake of Munro—"went missing."

"What'll you do?"

"I'll worry about that. You and the twins can thank me later for the cover story."

"Awright. S' good idea of yours," Cold said, sounding resentful.

Smith lurched off again, down a couple of steps and then forward, moving quickly. Munro opened his eyes enough to see the dirty, narrow street with the bedraggled houses jammed close and looming, blocking the light. Several children watched. He knew that if he called for help, no witness would come forward to help. If he vanished, the police would get nothing, not a word, from the inhabitants of this rookerie.

Another turn, and a third, and they apparently had passed the dead-ends and darkness.

Before Smith stepped into the sunshine of the street, he fumbled in his pockets and drew out a knife.

When Munro began to twist his body and pull his arms up, Smith hissed. "Stop. I'll drop you or stab you. No, I mean by accident, fool. Let me cut the rope."

The knife flashed at Munro's wrists, and his hands were free.

He nearly fell off Smith's shoulders in his eagerness to get on his own feet again.

"Hold up." Smith crouched, wincing, and cut the rope at Munro's ankles.

He straightened, and the knife vanished as quickly as it had appeared. Obviously, Smith practiced with that blade.

Munro yanked off the gag, then bent and grabbed the pieces of rope. He stood rubbing his wrists. The sun was sinking low in the sky, which meant it was past six o'clock.

"We're leaving. Act near dead in case we got witnesses. I'll drag you along."

Munro wanted to take off running, go to his friend Fairleigh looking for justice, like a child running to a nurse. Smith, who was several inches taller, slid an arm around his waist. Munro gasped when the pain hit.

"Don't grab me like that," he said in a low voice. "Your imbecilic friends might have cracked my rib."

He'd decided this was likely just a big bruise. But he'd use it as an excuse to escape Smith's hold.

Smith compromised by grabbing him by the arm as if marching him off to prison. As he'd hoped, the hold allowed Munro to reach into Smith's pocket. To cover the noise of crinkling paper, he said, "I remember how you were hauled about like a side of beef after your beating at Chester Street. Is this payback for that?"

"You might remember it." Smith looked up and down the street as he hauled Munro along. "I barely do." He took a moment to examine Munro. "But we talked about my debt, and that's more than erased. I'm saving your life like you saved mine. Another five minutes and we can be shot of each other."

"No. You can't go back to your father yet either. Come with me."

"To your imaginary house in the country?"

Munro had invented the pleasant fiction to lure him, but the house in Scotland was real. He felt mildly annoyed that Smith called him out as a liar just because he, uh, told a falsehood.

"At least give me a few hours of your time."

"What do you want?"

Munro didn't want to allow him to slip away. Now that he knew the other villains in the Smith circle were prone to violence, he'd rather stick with the devil he knew and not go looking for Joshua in their lair again.

He'd been a fool to agree to meet later and a bigger fool climbing over the wall. He'd paid for that mistake by hanging about and then getting captured and beaten. "Come with me, and I'll promise to tell no one about any of this. Not a word, unless you want me to spread the news that the Winter brothers kidnapped and planned to kill a policeman."

"That's a lie—you're not a cop." Smith sounded entirely indignant.

"That means that you lied to your friend Cold. You're not always so particular about the truth?"

"I'd expect you to be, Mr. Munro."

Munro looked at him sideways. "Why does it matter to you?"

"It doesn't."

"We do tend to squabble about silly things, have you noticed? Yet there is no point in arguing about this matter." Munro shrugged out of Smith's hold and shoved his hands into his pockets. "We need to find solutions that will suit us both, and I think that's possible."

"Solutions to what?"

"Your missing wife, for one."

"I'll make a deal with you, hey?" Smith held out a hand. "Give me back the paper you took from me, and I won't knock you out again."

Munro looked down at Smith's broad palm and decided to play for time. "I never did lose consciousness today. A few times, I wished I had."

Smith's hand didn't move. "I know when someone's dipped my pocket. And you're not much of a toolsman."

Munro sighed. "Come with me, and I'll give it back to you after we've talked."

"Where do you think I'd go with you?"

He ignored the incredulous sneering tone and answered, "My house. No one knows its location, not even the man I consider my closest friend in England."

Smith let his hand drop to his side. "Don't forget I have a knife."

"I won't forget that, or the fact that you outweigh me by at least two stone or that despite the injuries you suffered in the jail, you're in fine shape." He walked slightly faster, and Smith kept up. He didn't demand the letter Munro had taken.

Munro considered it a good sign that they'd reach some sort of agreement. The fact that he led a dangerous criminal to his home made his heart beat too quickly and hard, or perhaps it was a response to the danger he'd just escaped.

The tinge of anticipation coursing through him was likely brought on because he'd solve the case quickly—or so he told himself.

Chapter Seven

Joshua's curiosity won even though he usually did a good job of hiding that unwelcome bit of himself. Curious cats fared poorly in the Smith family.

His visit to the molly house had been his last idiotic episode, though it came more from yearning and a loneliness he could usually ignore. Now he recalled that itch easily because he felt it again. Sergeant Munro was just the sort of muscular, slender person he'd hungered for as long as he could recall such longings.

"Do you have any money?" Munro asked

He pulled out the leather bag that contained a few coins and held it up. "Why do you ask? Want to lift it too?"

"Your relations took all of mine."

"They might be family, but they're not my relations."

Munro gave him a puzzled look but only said, "I want to hire a hack because I can't keep walking. And I think you'd agree it's probably best not to be seen together, strolling along like friends."

As they limped toward a hansom cab, Munro said, "Do you see that I trust you now? I'm going to give this man my address and allow you to come with me. Does that not tell you I mean to do honestly by you?"

Joshua grunted. He'd had enough trying to understand the real meaning of this man's words and decided to just live in the moment instead of steps ahead. After all, if Munro came at him with a weapon, he had one of his own. He just wished the man didn't know the location of the Winters' flash-house—no matter that now he knew Munro's own bolt-hole.

The address Munro gave was not far from Piccadilly, far too fine for a cop. "Not the address most mutton-shunters could afford," Joshua pointed out.

Munro seemed to ignore him.

Joshua rarely rode in such a fast vehicle as the small and light hansom and decided he preferred the privacy of one of Big Mervin's creaking old carriages, fashioned from black Maria police wagons, one of Mervin's favorite jokes. The thing was well-sprung, though, and fairly skimmed over the cobblestones with only a few bounces and a little swaying.

They slowed for some crossing traffic just outside an exhibit of freaks with flags and sandwich-board men marching and calling nearby.

Munro glared at the fluttering colorful bunting. He made some sort of disgusted sound under his breath and a word that sounded like *frimse*.

Joshua jerked a thumb at the exhibit. "The Borneo boy and the fasting girl both are Neely's. You know that? Since you apparently work for him."

"Och, it's disgusting."

"Why do you say that?"

"Borneo boy is bad enough. At least he is an adult. But *feech*! That men should take a hungry or insane girl and turn her into an exhibition…"

Joshua shifted his feet, trying to stretch them out, but the small compartment kept him trapped. "They say Maisy hasn't eaten for months. Lives on air."

Munro gave a scornful laugh. "And you believe that nonsense about a girl living on air?"

Joshua shook his head. "Don't know what I believe, just know she's a good roper."

"A good what?"

"She'll bring in gawpers and then they'll come back to see if she's wasted to nothing. All the shillings she's bringing in, I wager Big Mervin will run a competitor, open his own gaff. Cheaper than a confidence man, and you can do it right out in the open."

"Utterly. Disgusting." Munro hitched away from him.

"No one's forced to pay money to see her. No one's forcing the girl to starve." After a moment, he added, "I think."

"Fech." It was the sound of a man clearing his throat.

Munro's indignation amused Joshua. Nicky had a word for the way Munro acted, and Joshua tried to scrape it up from his mind. "Sanctimony?" he said. "That's it. Sanctimonious."

They turned onto a tree-lined road that was almost as shadowy as the rookerie, but it smelled worlds better. Late evening sunlight shone in patches.

"No doubt you're correct," Munro said, sounding more English again. "But I worked hard for years to fight that sort of exploitation."

Joshua shrugged and gazed out the window. As always, he kept an eye open for familiar faces or aggressive postures. The world was a dangerous place, although you wouldn't think it, looking at these fine buildings.

The carriage stopped in front of a long row of houses. Each seemed almost as big and pretty as a terraced house Big Mervin once won in one of his gambling dens.

Big Mervin's temporary property had been on a quiet square in London, nothing like the rookerie or the warrens and warehouses Nick and Joshua had known all their lives.

For about a fortnight, they had run wild, even mostly grown Nick, thumping up and down wide staircases and sliding on polished floors until Big Mervin sold it back to the unlucky gambler's family for an enormous sum. The sale must have been a relief for the neighbors—but not for Joshua. Living with his father in those clean uncluttered rooms had seemed a special time.

Munro's house brought back that house and time as if years had been peeled away. Could it be the same square? He looked across the grass, through the wrought iron fence into the little green park. No, that square had been wider and had a fountain in the middle.

Joshua could recognize the air of wealth here, and it brought back all the times in the Smith family when great sums of money came in a flash and vanished near as quick. Not for Big Mervin, of course, but he lived separate from them all. King Mervin, Nick had called him. Only when he was older did Joshua understand that the phrase wasn't meant to be a compliment.

The white granite row he looked at now was not as top-of-the-trees as it had seemed at first. The sounds of singing and piano music drifted from one open window, and the scent of cigar smoke came from another.

"Pardon." Munro's voice interrupted his look round. "I don't have the fare for the driver."

"Right." He dug some coins from the bag and handed them over.

As Munro fiddled with the front door lock, Joshua reclaimed his letter from the detective's coat pocket unnoticed. Their own private game of pass the potato, he thought with some amusement, as he slid the paper into his inside pocket.

"No servants?" he asked as the door swung open.

"At the moment, I have a housekeeper and maid, neither of whom are here. If I stay, I'll probably hire more staff."

"You have a nice setup. You still haven't told me how this came to be. Maybe you met plenty who could ready the rozzer," Joshua said.

"That means bribery, I think?" Munro seemed interested rather than affronted. He closed the front doors.

"Perhaps."

"I inherited this house."

"Did you? Huh." Joshua believed him but wanted to see how far he could push before Munro lost his temper.

"Indeed, I did."

"Maybe you have been piggoting to cover your tracks," Joshua tried.

"Piggoting means lying? What an interesting word. Do you happen to know its origin?"

Joshua gave up his attempt to needle the man. Since he wasn't offered a tour, he decided to take one of his own and began to walk through the empty foyer. He brushed past Munro, who gave a little gasp as their arms touched.

"Afraid?" Joshua asked.

Munro didn't answer, so Joshua went to a broad entrance guarded by double doors and tried the handle. It opened, and he walked into a large room with most of the furniture hidden under shrouds of cloth.

He turned to Munro, who stood in the doorway. "I thought you lived here?"

Munro wiped a hand over his jaw. "I do. This room is cold. The kitchen has a huge monster of a range, and it keeps the back of the house nicely warm—or a misery on hot days, I suppose. I haven't lived here long enough to know if that's true or not. The only time I visited was as a child."

He explained himself too much. Maybe when Munro got uncomfortable, he babbled.

Joshua hadn't made Munro angry, but he'd made him good and nervous. That was so unlike anything he'd seen in the man, he wondered why.

Then it came to him and he tried the idea out loud. "You're jumpy because of Chester Street, aren't you?" He took a step forward and Munro backed away. Confirmation. "You're worried that I want you."

Munro didn't answer. He wet his lips with his tongue. After a long moment, the truth slammed home into Joshua, who only blinked. That wasn't *just* fear haunting Munro.

The realization seemed to come to Munro as well, and astound him nearly as much. And then he had to deny it to them both, naturally. He folded his arms and backed up. "Nonsense," he said. "No. I'm absolutely fine. And you're no threat even with that knife."

Joshua grinned at him.

"Stop it," Munro ordered.

"Stop it or what?" Joshua's smile broadened. He would never have this conversation with the men in the Smith family. Probably he wouldn't speak in this manner with anyone but Munro, who was not a cop and really not a threat. He could needle the man and at the same time admit the truth about himself. "You'll call the police and have me thrown out? Maybe thrown in jail again? You invited me here. Insisted I come along with you. If you want more than just conversation, let me know, eh?"

He walked past Munro into the hall, trying as hard as he could to keep the lurch out of his step and the spring of hope out of his chest.

He guessed the way to the kitchen correctly. The cast iron range wasn't too hot but just warm enough that he wanted to pull off his jacket. He could see a bit of a glow through the slits on the front.

Munro again lurked in the doorway.

Joshua dragged out a chair from the big wooden table and sat near the stove. "If you didn't want to talk about pleasure, what did you want to talk about? Hmm?"

Munro's hand dove into his pocket, and then his other pockets.

Joshua held up the paper. "This what you're looking for?"

Munro stormed into the kitchen, but Joshua was faster. He leaned to the range, used the grate handle to lever open the cast iron door, and dropped the paper in.

Munro's response was nothing like he'd expected. After a long, stunned moment, he clapped a hand on Joshua's shoulder and began to laugh.

"This has been the longest day of my life." Munro walked past him, grabbed another chair, and placed it near him. Not so close the chairs touched, but not across the room either.

Then he walked to a far cupboard and took down two glasses and a decanter of some sort. "I am bruised and battered and terrorized by your family. I have almost no answers and very little to take back to my employer. And worse, I am worried about a young woman no one else seems to care about." He poured out two glasses, walked back to Joshua, and handed him one.

He still rubbed his side, wincing. When he took a sip, he gave a sharp cry and put down the glass. "M'muof," he said, gingerly touching the corner of his lips.

"The gag," Joshua said.

Munro nodded then gulped much of the rest of his glass with only a gasp showing the discomfort.

Joshua took a small sip. He didn't know anything other than beer, wine, and gin. This was like wine but less harsh.

Munro leaned back in the chair and heaved a sigh. "I'd be more worried about not finding Mrs. Smith, but after spending some hours in your company, I suspect three things." He held up a finger. "If the lady was in grave danger or dead, you'd be less sanguine. I don't think you're indifferent to her as you appear." He held up another finger. "You're as slippery as an eel, and your sense of fun is as criminal as your family's concerns."

He fell silent, and Joshua reached over and gave his leg a nudge. "The third?"

"You know where she is. You destroyed that letter—and I'm convinced it was from her—but you know the important facts such as her address. Why did you burn it?"

"No reason to keep it."

"Don't you worry that someone will claim you murdered her? That letter to you would prove you're not involved. I'm assuming it was sent from somewhere other than London."

Joshua couldn't help rolling his eyes. "I'm not telling you where it's from."

"But my other point. You'd need some evidence—"

"Did you just arrive in town yesterday, Munro? I've got no need for protection. There'd be witnesses to claim I was with them on whatever day she'd died."

Munro looked alarmed.

Joshua took another swallow. The alcohol was finer than any he'd drunk. He supposed after he'd just admitted he was bent, as crooked at the rookerie's alley, he should reassure Munro. "She's not dead, far as I know."

"Good." Munro stretched his arms high, wincing again. But his long arms and lean body drew most of Joshua's attention.

He got up to fetch the decanter, and Joshua watched. Those broad shoulders and long arms and legs seemed as elegant as any woman's, but elegant was too fancy a word for all that muscle and bone.

Munro brought over the liquor and poured some in each of their glasses.

He sat, then stared at Joshua with unnerving attention with those light eyes, which seemed a cold gray at the moment. "You won't tell me where your wife is, but you should know that she might be in danger. I'm not the only one who's looking for her."

"Oh?"

"There were men—I speak of men other than those thuggish friends of yours who grabbed me—who were watching your apartment. Did you see them?"

Joshua shrugged.

Munro sat back again and shifted his attention to the glass in his hand. "I think they were... I think that her father hired them."

The way he paused interested Joshua. What was he about to say before he changed his mind?

Joshua asked, "Did your Mr. Kelly hire others?"

"If he did, he didn't confide in me."

Joshua finished his drink and put his glass on the table, a little harder than he'd meant to. "Were you trying to catch a look at those other watchers when the Winters grabbed you?"

Munro smiled and shook his head slowly back and forth.

"Is that a no?"

"Ach, you're right. I was trying to see who was watching the watchers. A silly day." He drank down his wine. The pain at the corners of his mouth didn't seem to bother him now. And there he was again, staring at Joshua as if he could see through his face into his brainpan. Once Nick had taken Joshua to a fire-and-brimstone church, and that preacher had stared at each worshiper in the pews in turn with just such passion. He didn't seem to be searching for the people but deep into them, hunting for their souls, much good that did his congregation that was hungry for food, not salvation. Munro was talking again. "Do you know much of the reason I pitied you in jail?"

Because you're a good person, better than that preacher. Joshua wondered why that thought popped into his nut, and what it meant. Nothing good.

Munro filled his glass again. "I thought you were slow. I thought, there's a poor boy brought in to entertain the gentlemen and he likely has no other way to make his way in the world, and here are the police turning ugly to a man with a child's mind."

Joshua laughed.

"Yes, I was disabused of that notion quickly enough. No need to remind me that your family name is well-known to everyone in the police force but myself. And you're not a halfwit after all. Is that what's amusing you?"

Joshua had laughed so hard that he had to wipe his eyes. "Sure." He sniffed and hiccupped. "And that I'm pretty enough to be a whore? I don't think so."

"Not every man who visits such a house is looking for a pretty young thing. There's the appeal of—of someone more manly as well."

"And you'd know this how?"

"I saw all the occupants of the Chester Street house." The answer came too quickly. "And from what I could tell, from what I heard, the place was used for assignations, not only by professional whores." He folded his arms high over his chest and winced again.

"Your side hurts?" Joshua asked. "Should I look at it?"

Munro ignored him. "Were you there for an assignation?"

Joshua told himself often enough after that night that he would not be embarrassed. Shame was a weakness, and he had no room for that in his world. He had no need to answer any of these questions either. But he did. "To meet up with someone in particular, you mean? No."

"Had you gone before?"

"I answered questions like this already. No and no, and no again. Or yes, if that's the proper answer."

"No, no. I don't ask because of my former profession."

"Then why?"

"Curiosity." The word came out in a voice as soft as Joshua's own. "I wondered if it was…" His voice trailed off.

No way Joshua would push him to talk about this.

"Never mind," Munro said.

"Do you want to know if it was a good time?" Joshua prompted.

Munro waved a hand.

"Why'd you ask?" Joshua tried a different version of the question. There was a set to Munro's face that he didn't trust. "Are you going to sneak into a whorehouse?"

"I'd think paying for that sort of, ahem, attention would be a sad debasement of real affection."

Preacher Munro was rising to the surface.

Joshua lifted his right hand and waggled his fingers. "This is the sad affection I usually get."

Munro sputtered something indignant about disgusting obscenity, but a moment later began to guffaw. The man was a treat, a combination of prudishness and fun.

Joshua leered at him. "You've never done the same? Never brought yourself off? I don't believe you."

Munro's face went red. "Frequent emissions are unhealthy."

"You're blushing. Funny response for a policeman. You've seen what people get up to."

"I'm not blushing." He sipped his wine. "And at any rate, where I'm from, people don't get up to much more than some thievery and assault with only a touch of the lewd and only on occasion. I only came to London recently a few months ago. I was a visiting sergeant, courtesy of a program my friend at the new criminal investigation division attempted. Bloody Fairleigh," he added.

Joshua snorted. "That branch." Big Mervin hated them.

Munro must have read his mind. "I expect your father was sad to see those corrupt detectives caught and forced out."

Joshua didn't like the fact that the conversation was sliding from the interesting sort of talk that tightened his insides, to the dull business of his father's work. But before he could push the talk to lewd again, Munro was speaking.

"And after my performance, I don't suppose they'll allow another visiting sergeant." He'd gone gloomy. Now the preacher's eyes had become the penitent's.

"What went wrong?" Joshua asked.

The question seemed to amuse Munro, and that was pretty, the way his smile lit those eyes and he had just the hint of a dimple on his cheek. Joshua was so distracted by that smile, he almost missed the words. "*You* did. There was a great deal of resentment about the special treatment I gave you. Or so they said. That's one reason I left my position. Another was I grew tired of living in the special section house at the station."

Joshua homed in on one phrase he'd used. "Special treatment?"

"Yes. After the fact, I was given to understand that in your case, any medical intervention at all meant something special." He gave a humorless laugh. "And there were plenty of innuendoes as well after I fell asleep in your presence."

"You slept? I don't remember." And wasn't that a pity.

"This isn't worth discussing."

"It is. Go on."

"I shouldn't have paid such close attention to you. I wasn't forced from my job, but staying was dashed uncomfortable."

"Any attention to someone nabbed in that house is cause for trouble?"

"I supposed. Yet my troubles weren't entirely because I was what they called 'overkind' to someone discovered in the Chester Street raid."

"Ah. My last name?"

"Yes. Being the son of Mervin Smith might have saved your life in that jail, but it ended my time on the metropolitan police force." Munro swallowed more wine and absently touched the corner of his mouth, which no longer looked cracked or red. "Apparently, some on the met resent your father more than they enjoy his bribes. They'd like to see him suffer."

"They don't know Big Mervin, then."

Munro raised his eyebrows. "What do you mean by that?"

"He'd be put out if I were to fall off the twig, but it would hardly be punishment." Joshua absently rubbed his aching leg. "That's his strength. He doesn't hold tight to affection."

"How is that a strength?"

"If he can't be rattled by the death of family or friends, it's harder to work him from outside."

"Good God, not allowing true connections in life can hardly be considered a gift to him or anyone close to him. I'm so sorry. It's cruelty."

Joshua shrugged. "It's business."

The earnestness of Munro was too strong. Likely he'd had too much to drink and would regret getting missish now. If they were to do something to regret, why couldn't they return to talk of grasping pegos and perhaps playing backgammon? Once before he died, he'd like to try all the pleasure he'd dreamed of—as Munro would swear, *by God.*

"Do you strive to be the same?" Munro asked.

Ah, he was speaking of Big Mervin's ability to easily let go.

Joshua had tried to be like his father for years, until Nicky's body was pulled from the Thames. "Don't think so," he said. "Not sure I can," he added with a bit of regret.

Munro leaned forward, moving carefully. He tilted sideways. Before he could go all preachish again, Joshua asked, "You're moving slow. That rib?"

"Yes. But I don't believe it's broken."

"Let me see." Joshua made it a mild demand. Too strong and he'd seem overeager. Too weak and Munro would ignore him again.

Munro rose to his feet and hauled his shirt out of his trousers. He left his braces on and didn't undo his trousers. Standing still, he held up his shirt, his body canted to the side to show off his injury.

Joshua released a whoosh of air. He'd been desperate enough to hold his breath as he waited to see the texture of Munro's skin, to see if there was hair on his torso. His skin was pale but not as fish-belly gray as the usual Londoner. The dark hair on his stomach and chest was sparse, the bruise on his side already huge and purple.

Joshua wet his lips and leaned closer, trying to peek at more. Disgusting perversion, but he felt so full of that giddy anticipation, he barely cared.

"Well?" Munro asked.

"Eh. Um. You can pull in a big breath?" Joshua knew too well that broken ribs meant breathing could be a horror.

Munro nodded.

Joshua scooted his chair closer and carefully traced his fingers on the warm skin near the bruise. "That hurt?" He let his touch linger at the base of the bruise, not far from Munro's hipbone. Another bruise bloomed near his small nipple. Joshua's own nipples seemed to tighten as he reached to touch the mark. "You bruise easy."

"That I do. It's fine. I'll be fine." His voice had a touch of a quaver.

Their breathing was loud in the nearly silent kitchen. Munro lowered the shirt too soon. But he did unbutton his trousers to tuck it away again.

Joshua had touched other men's cocks, two to be exact, but he hadn't seen a naked man up close, and he wanted a chance. The glimpses of patrons with women at Smith's whorehouse didn't count. He wanted a private display just for him, and he wanted this man to provide it.

He longed to see Munro in the altogether and would use underhanded means to reach his goal. He wrinkled his nose and raised an eyebrow, an exaggerated look of disgust. It wasn't entirely falsehood, for as he'd dragged Munro out, he'd caught the scent of coal and rat piss and the sweat of fear. He said, "You got a washtub? If you're feeling poorly, I can help you heat some water for a bath, help you set one up."

Munro gave a snort. "Not a subtle hint."

Uh-oh, he'd been found out.

"I'm well aware I don't smell fresh as flowers."

Good. Munro had no notion of what he wanted after all. "I've smelled sweeter things," Joshua drawled. No point in adding that he'd smelled far, far worse.

"I'll bathe after we have a plan in place."

Joshua's plans were simple: touch Munro and maybe do more. Later on—after he could get his brain to operate somewhere other than behind the fly of his trousers—he'd think about tomorrow. He'd have to answer to Big Mervin about Munro by then.

"Tell me the contents of that letter," Munro continued. "Tell me where Mrs. Smith is located."

Joshua could have lied. He should have. "No."

"You know I don't work for anyone who would hurt her."

"Kelly, you said. Neely, I think. Take me to meet your employer, and I'll talk to him."

Munro shook his head. "No." His turn to be brief.

"Then we have no deal." Joshua settled back in the comfortable chair. He hadn't known a plain wooden kitchen chair could be so luxurious. The servants in this place lived well.

"Alas, you force me to explain myself." Munro poured still more wine. "I don't wish to speak to Kelly at the moment. And I'm putting off visiting her father as well."

"You haven't seen Neely?"

"No. What is your impression of the man?"

"I never talked to him."

"He wasn't at the wedding?"

Joshua shook his head.

"Interesting. Did his daughter seem upset about that?"

"Yes. She seemed upset." She had seemed terrified.

"I want to wait to speak to Neely until I understand the situation better," Munro said. "That means you are my only lead in this case."

"You don't want to talk to Kelly because you're planning to charge him more for the job? Oh, do you want to hold Matilda hostage or just dig out information about her? Get Neely and Kelly into a bidding war over her? I'll wager that last won't work."

Munro snorted. "I don't operate in the same manner as your family, Mr. Smith. I wish to ascertain exactly what the lady wants before I talk to anyone else. The same action I think you indicated you're taking."

Joshua wondered if Munro wasn't very clever after all. "No need for you to do that. I made it clear I'll find out what she wants without your help."

"You apparently don't even know why she fled or who she fears."

"Do you?"

"I'd thought it was you, but I don't any longer."

That comment should have made Joshua sputter indignantly that he was a fearful cove, but he only grinned at Munro. Being a monster might be good for Smith business, but it warmed him to hear Munro didn't think him one. Joshua asked, "Any other notions, then?"

"You're not telling, are you?"

Joshua shrugged.

"Here is what I know: you apparently wish to send a letter and wait for a reply. She's obviously not in London, or you'd get an answer back sooner than four days. I don't want to wait four days. I'd like to get on a train as soon as possible and go find the lady and talk to her."

"What's the hurry? Do you need your pay fast?" He looked around. "Ever thought of selling a few knickknacks?"

"No, no, no. It's not a matter of finances." Munro's voice went a bit singsong again, as if he battled impatience. "I think there is something going on that you either don't know about or aren't willing to discuss."

Joshua shrugged again. "Why the hurry?"

"It makes me uneasy to think of her out in the world, without protection from the wolves. Unless you've managed to set up protection as well?"

Joshua didn't know the woman, beyond the time they'd been together during and after the wedding. This man didn't know her at all. It seemed strange Munro would go to so much trouble for someone he hadn't even met—and wasn't even sure of his pay to rescue her.

"Why do you care?"

Munro scratched his jaw, which showed the start of pale stubble. "I doubt anyone else can truly understand, but I am... It is important to me to help this woman."

"Some sort of vow you took?" Joshua thought of his peculiar wedding.

"Yes. That's as good an explanation as any."

The man's eyes were haunted. Someone or something from his past nagged at Munro. Joshua would push that story later. "I didn't know anyone to send to keep her safe. And truth is, she might not be where I think she is." He wasn't sure if he was bothered more by Matilda's silence or this man's judgment.

"All the more reason to go to the place, wherever it might be, and check." Munro frowned at Joshua as if he were seeing a puddle of puke and not a man. "Isn't she with child?"

Joshua almost said *not mine*, but he didn't think Munro would think that was important. He didn't want to look bad in those preacher's eyes and for some reason, he suspected that would draw the glare. He just nodded. "Far along too."

"How far?"

"I'm no midwife. No idea."

"And it's not yours?"

"Sergeant Munro, remember where I'd been the night we met."

Munro turned pink, but he didn't back down. "Some men are interested in any willing body, male or female."

"Know that from your own interests?"

Munro's expression shifted from disgust to flat-out horror. When he tilted his chin up, he showed that fine jawline and firm chin. "See here, this has nothing to do with finding your wife."

"No," Joshua agreed. "But it's fun to see you stiffen as if there was a rod jammed up your arse."

"Your idea of fun is not mine."

"That's a pity," Joshua said.

Munro went red again. He sniffed in hard, then let out the breath slowly, as if calming himself. "So you think your *wife* is close to her time." He put a strong emphasis on that word wife, but sounded even-tempered enough.

"Yes." Joshua smiled at him, even as he gave up trying to either annoy or fuck this man. The first didn't entertain him after all—Munro wouldn't play along. The second wasn't in the cards. "And yes, she wrote me a note. It said she had help. Figured it was the man who put that bun in the oven."

"What else did she say?"

"She apologized." Which was actually more than he'd deserved. The other lines came to him. *I'm sure you'd be a good husband to someone, and I hope you are not upset, but, at the moment I fled, I had no other answers. I still don't know what else I could have done.*

He said, "She wrote well enough. Neely must have made sure she got a bit of education. Or someone did."

Like Nicky did for me, he thought.

Big Mervin had wanted his boys to talk properly and read, in case they could be used for the family's plans to break into the world where the real money lay. Nicky had taught his little half brother Joshua under orders—but he'd cared. Cared too much, came the automatic thought.

This Munro reminded him of a tougher version of Nicky. A shadow of mercy lay over the hard man.

Joshua got up and poured himself another glass of wine or whatever it was. If he couldn't get his hands on Munro, he might as well plan.

His father had sent the Winters after him, but Joshua considered the slate between his father and himself nearly wiped clean with all the goods and the apartment he'd hand over to Mervin.

He'd kept track of the score and knew he didn't owe anyone anything, not information, not loyalty, not money, and that was a giddy thought. And if he gave this man a few words, he'd have Munro in his debt, an even better one.

"Some village in Derbyshire," he said. "Merlswell, wherever that is."

"A market town near Glossop. Near the Peaks."

"How do you know about it?"

"I like looking at maps."

Joshua wasn't sure he'd ever seen a proper map. He put down his glass and pointed at Munro. "So. That's what I know."

"*Is* that everything? What was the name of the inn?"

"Don't think I'll tell you more than that for now."

Munro rose slowly to his feet. Joshua wondered if he was going to ask him to go now that he'd gotten what he required from him. "I'll go bathe, then. And we can go buy our train tickets."

"What makes you think I'll go with you?"

"What else will you do? And I'll pay your fare."

"I might go back to my father. They're expecting you." It occurred to him then. "You just don't want me going back and telling the others you're still on this side of a dirt bed."

"You come with me," Munro said. "Because it's your wife we're talking about."

That shouldn't have made a difference. Except a moment later, Joshua found himself nodding. "I'll go. I'll help. You give me a cut of what Kelly offered."

Munro's gaze traveled up and down his body, his eyes filled with weary disgust. Again.

Joshua raised his hands in surrender. "I didn't know the woman. It was just a marriage our fathers arranged for their own reasons. I'm not even sure of those."

"Never mind those men. What about you? Didn't you swear an oath? To preserve and protect?"

He had nothing to say to that. "Take a bath. I'll help fill the tub."

"No need. There's a tub upstairs in a bathroom."

"Indeed? With taps and all?"

"One tap that works. The pipes to hot water were never connected, so my grandfather had hot water hauled upstairs, but there's plenty of cold to be had up there. I won't be long. Feel free to look for food if you wish."

In the end, Joshua didn't get to see Munro's body. He considered just barging into the bathroom and seeing what that got him. After all, in the Smith family, not taking what you wanted was considered weakness. Restraint was only good if you kept your eye on a future prize.

Yes, that was why he kept himself in the kitchen by the fire, eating a chunk of pork pie and drinking the excellent liquor. He licked a bit of crust from his knuckle and thought about the man upstairs, naked and shivering in cold water, wishing he could explore that chilly skin with his hands and tongue. He'd wait because he had plans.

He'd seen desire in Munro. Now Munro just had to admit it to himself. Once he was honest to them both, Joshua might take what he craved.

Chapter Eight

Munro had only a few suits to choose from. It took time to get used to having enough money, and he still hadn't gone to a tailor. He hurriedly buttoned his shirt, trousers, braces, then the blue wool waistcoat. The shirt collar wouldn't attach right, so he threw it away and tried with another. Once he did get to a tailor, he'd get shirts with collars and hang the laundering expense.

The basic black tie wouldn't tie properly, and his gray tweed made him look a little gray himself, but why the devil would he fret over his appearance when he should be considering his plans?

Go north. Find Mrs. Smith. Not so very difficult for a detective.

He filled his pockets with the watch, a billfold, and a handy foldable knife. His larger knife went on his sock's suspender. He slipped that in place before tying the brogues. They were going to tramp around the country.

He would be glad to get away from London in the early spring. He grabbed a valise and jammed in shirts, underclothing, and another suit and closed it quickly. There wasn't any real reason to rush, but he had a sense that Smith wouldn't wait for him before disappearing into his maze of alleys and warehouses of London.

And would that be the worst thing? Now that he had a location, he could search for the lady on his own. It was hardly a huge metropolis. There couldn't be more than a few inns in that market town, and a lady traveling alone, especially one so near her time, would be someone they'd notice. Still, he hurriedly latched the valise and then thumped down the stairs as if trying to get to Smith before he sneaked out of the house.

Smith sat in the kitchen with an empty plate in front of him. Munro's own stomach growled.

He went into the pantry and grabbed the heel of bread. "All right. We'll go in a few minutes."

Smith rose to his feet, taller than Munro recalled yet again. He was the sort of man who seemed to be taller or shorter depending on the expression he wore or how he shifted his body. He'd be a good actor, Munro thought. Perhaps that was the secret of Smith senior's success: the ability to make himself into something larger than life. Munro had heard Big Mervin could convey power and threat beyond simple acts of violence. After all, he acted as a commander of his strange army. And how close to that seat of power was Joshua Smith? He'd find out, he supposed.

Munro went to the study and got a pen and paper.

"Who you writing to?" That rough voice came from close by his side, and Munro grew aware of Smith's chest rising and falling with each breath.

"Housekeeper." He capped the well with a reasonably steady hand and straightened up. After wiping the pen, he carried the note to the front hall, where he left all communication with the household staff—the two people he rarely talked to.

"Gimme paper and pen too."

"You write?"

"Of course. The family will want an answer about you. Don't want them coming after either of us, eh?"

"What will you tell them?"

"I'll say I've taken care of you and am following a hint you gave me about some business. That'll be enough to hold them for a time. I hope."

"Taken care of?" Munro asked. "Will they think that means murdered?"

Smith looked up at him, laughter in those dark eyes. How had he ever thought them stupid? Smith touched the end of his pen, stroked it. "I can take care of you another better way, if you want."

Munro hurried off, leaving him chuckling over the note he was writing. When Smith joined him, Munro grabbed a hat and jammed it on his still-damp hair, and stopped to look in the mirror on the giant umbrella holder and hat rack in the hall.

Munro wasn't the only one examining his image. Smith looked Munro up and down with a bit of a smile on his face, as if he approved of what he saw.

"We might stop so you can pick up some clothes," he began.

"Neither of us want to go back to the apartment or to the warren."

"Warren? Where's that?"

As usual, Smith ignored a question he didn't want to answer. "Use the rest of my coins. If it isn't enough, you're buying my ticket. And some ready-made clothing along the way. Your mysterious Mr. Kelly can pay."

"Yes, don't fret yourself. I shall fund this trip." Munro walked out the door with the sensation of excitement one got at the start of a holiday. It was getting out of London, of course.

Traveling with Mr. Smith had nothing to do with it.

At the station, he bought two tickets in first class. He'd usually gone second or third class until his grandfather's death gave him the funds he'd needed to take first. Smith visited the mail office in the station and found him again by the train, his hat pulled low over his face.

"Any reason you appear so nervous?" Munro asked.

"Some of these boys who grab luggage work for Big Mervin," he said.

The platform was crowded, and Munro had assumed they wouldn't be alone in the train, but apparently, Smith's scowl and limp were enough to drive away anyone walking to the cars. Smith scanned the crowds continuously as he waited for Munro to open the door to the compartment.

When they settled onto the worn but comfortable leather bench seats across from each other, Smith didn't speak but only gazed out the window with what appeared to be fascination. He hadn't seemed worried in the station, only his usual careful self. Now he was edgy, his shoulders hunched high.

And when the train jolted to a start, Smith also gave a jerk. He took off his hat. He put it back on.

"You're nervous." Munro probably shouldn't have sounded so amazed, but the thought struck him as bizarre. This man seemed unafraid of anything…other than rats, he reminded himself. "Is this your first time on a train?"

Smith wiped a hand at the window, as if he could erase the dirt on the smeary glass to see better.

"No." Smith used his coat sleeve on the glass. It didn't help. "I went on one ages ago and don't much recall it. Just not used to trains is all."

"How can that be?"

"I stay in London." He eased back on the seat, still staring out the window. "How fast are we going now?"

"Maybe twenty miles per hour? It will reach speeds of fifty."

Smith pressed his lips together. "Oh. I thought it would be... My brother..."

He broke off.

"Your brother? Do you mean Nicholas?"

"Never mind."

"We're here for hours. You might as well tell me."

Smith smiled, such an unexpected bright expression on that face. "My brother said trains could go two hundred miles an hour."

"Why on earth would he say something like that?"

"Don't have brothers, do you?"

"No, but I expect I understand your meaning." Munro was amused despite himself. "What else did your brother tell you?"

The smile turned into a scowl even darker than usual.

"To pass the time," Munro said. "Why not tell me what it is like to be Mervin Smith's son? Or Nicholas Smith's brother."

Smith closed his eyes. "I'll sleep."

"Very well." Munro pulled out a book and tried to read, but the train soon pulled onto a less smooth track, and the jounces made concentrating on the words in his lap difficult.

From across the way came Smith's soft, gruff voice. "He taught me to read. Do numbers, say m'prayers, and best way to palm or dip."

"Steal from people and shops?"

Smith said, "He was small and one of the best. I got too big. Played the part of distraction. And occasional rougher bits too."

"A hunter? A nobbler?" Munro asked. He hoped he used the right words for a smash-and-grab man and a criminal bully-man.

90

Smith only shrugged. He did that often, bringing Munro's attention to those shoulders. Munro waited, but Smith only sat with his head tilted to the side, his eyes closed.

A sleepy Smith might be more open to speaking of things that mattered, so Munro leaned close and tried, "Do you miss him?"

Smith gave a single half nod, which Munro would have missed if he hadn't been watching very carefully.

"What happened to him?"

The silence stretched, and Munro was just thinking of trying to read again when Smith spoke. His voice was low as usual, so Munro had to lean forward to hear. He tried to ignore the fillip he felt deep inside when he caught Smith's already familiar scent. He'd draw close just to hear the words, he reminded himself.

"He got hurt, stopped earning his way," Smith said. "Annoyed the wrong people with talk of mercy and goodness."

"Did he find religion?"

"Not so much." His sigh came as a wash of breath against Smith's cheek. "Fell for a female. Which is a kind of worship, maybe. Though he did have more God and so on than some. We all know the Bible."

"How's that?"

Smith opened his eyes again and stared at him for a long moment. "Someone told Big Mervin the coppers act less aggressive in places with Bibles in them. He had Bibles installed everywhere."

"Does he believe some sort of magical protection is at work?"

"Dunno." Smith shifted away from him and looked out the window.

"What happened to the female? The one your brother fell for?"

Smith's gaze didn't shift. He cleared his throat. "Dead. Same as Nicky. Dead." His voice was a bit louder now.

"Did you know her well?"

He shrugged, then said, "Yes. How long do we stay on this train?"

"You're not very subtle when you try to change the subject."

91

He gave a husky laugh. It reminded Munro of a lion's chuff. "I don't need to be. How long?"

"It's another four hours, I'd say."

Smith stretched out his long legs, pressing his hand over the area on his thigh above the bone that had been broken. Munro watched Smith's broad palm rubbing back and forth, his fingers kneading. Then the motion became positively...suggestive. When he glanced up, he saw Smith watched him, a wide grin on his face.

A hot rush of annoyance filled Munro. Then he understood he was feeling emotions deeper and more disturbing than fury—a fascination with Smith—and he grew even angrier. He lifted his book in front of his face.

"You going to give up being a copper altogether, then?" Smith asked, calm as could be.

"Probably." Munro risked glancing at Smith's hand, which rested on his leg, no longer moving.

Smith leaned forward and tapped his knee, one of Munro's own tricks. "Why's that?"

Munro hauled in a long breath to calm himself. He thought about Fairleigh's comment about how Munro had run away. He supposed the way he couldn't remain tranquil, especially around this man, could be reason enough to quit the force. "If I were a cop in a place where the work was bearable, I'd have to work in a village again. You can't get away with treating people like garbage in a community where everyone knows everyone else. People talk. Whereas the city is anonymous."

Smith gave another grunt of laughter. "Not my city," he explained. "I know more'n a hundred folk. And see 'em all the time."

Munro thought about it. "Yes, there are indeed neighborhoods. I suppose the police force is yet such another neighborhood. Which means I wouldn't have had an easy time anywhere in the Met because I got the reputation as that blasted pudding-hearted Scot."

"Because you saved me."

"That as well as other reasons."

"That big house you inherited?" Smith said.

Munro didn't bother to answer. The clack and rattle of the train filled the silence. After a full minute, Smith said, "Thank you for helping me." His smile was gone. "I haven't said that, have I?"

"Last time I saw you in jail, you were unable to speak."

"I barely can now."

"Certainly you can. There's a gravelly note, but you're better able to speak than any number of other Londoners. That is to say, I can understand you. So many of the folk from the East End gabble streams of words I can't grasp. You barely have a trace of cockney."

Smith's passing scowl and darkness vanished. He certainly had an expressive face. "Big Mervin wanted us to be at least as good as anyone in service. Nick talked like a banker, even."

"Aha, he wanted you to do inside work?"

His smile was wicked, and the scar under his eye curved with it. "He told me I got the reputation for steadiness."

"You can control yourself, aye? You don't rage and froth like that Cold person? No drinking yourself into a stupor come payday?"

Smith folded his arms. "I expect the boyos call me dull when out of my hearing."

The undercurrent of something dangerous remained, but it was inside Munro himself, not Smith. He realized he liked Smith's steadiness of character—or at least his semblance of that. Of course, the most violent man Munro had ever dealt with never shouted or made threats. He just pulled out his knife and cut throats. He'd best recall that man's outward calm when he dealt with Smith.

The gentleman from his past would visit him in his worst dreams. Smith had already barged into one of his best, not that he'd ever admit as much to anyone else.

"You all right?" Smith leaned forward. "You look like you got the morbs."

The man was too observant. Munro said, "I'm making a plan about what we should do when we arrive." Yes, that would be a good idea.

"Oh, what's best, do you think?"

"I think we shouldn't stay together and you might avoid showing yourself. Your wife might recognize you and run away if you approach. Whereas I could make enquiries at the inn without raising suspicion."

"Hmm."

Munro thought about the notes he'd gotten from Kelly. "I don't have a good likeness of her. It's been a few years since she sat for a photograph." He pulled a picture from his pocket, a tintype. "Does this look like her?"

Smith frowned down at it. "Sure. Maybe." He sounded dubious. "I think her face was thinner than this. Older. She wasn't big anywhere but in the middle."

He touched himself on the chin. "She came up to about here."

"You're six feet something?"

Smith shrugged. "Dunno."

"Is her hair straight? Curling? It's hardly more than a dark blob in that old photograph."

"A bit frizzy, I'd say," Smith said. "And all piled on the back of her head. A lot of it. In a braid."

"In other words, she looks like nearly any other young woman of nineteen."

"With a bigger belly. Unless she's whelped already. A month at least has passed."

"That long? They've waited that long to find her? Didn't anyone come to you to ask where she was? Other than your lot, I mean."

Smith's gaze was steady. "Maybe your Mr. Kelly had been in touch with her."

"No, no. Ach, damme, I might as well tell you, he's not acquainted with her. He was hired to find her and set me on the job. He has too much work and farms it out to others."

"He's not the baby's father."

"No. Not likely."

"Wonder why he'll pay to get her found. I mean, what's the profit in tracking down the girl?"

94

"It's not all about profit and loss."

Smith narrowed his eyes at him. "Sure it is. Anyone who tells you else is lying."

"You sound like you're repeating the words of a catechism. You haven't stopped to examine the meaning for a long time. Or perhaps ever."

Smith eyed him long and hard. "Examining meaning is a gentleman's hobby. And only a man who's made his packet can indulge."

That also sounded like he was parroting someone else's words.

"It's a tough road you follow," Munro said sadly.

"I'm not on any road, except to Derbyshire." He leaned his head back against the lace-and-linen antimacassar.

"And when we return?"

"I'll go to Big Mervin."

"Don't you wish to be done with him?"

"And do what instead? I have a bad leg, no voice, no training for anything but his sort of business." He closed his eyes. "It could be worse. I could be m'brother."

"Who died of caring too much."

His mouth quirked up just a little. "That's it exactly, Mr. Munro."

"What will your father do if he discovers you plan to help your wife?"

"Did I say I would help her?"

"Why else would you be taking this journey? Mr. Smith, I don't know you well, but I'd bet a tenner that you are not bloodthirsty."

"I'm not a fool either."

"Hmm." He didn't intend anything other than agreement by the sound, but Smith took it as a rebuttal.

"Fine. But you're another one, tracking a woman you've never met and who might have other dangerous types after her. You won't get pay enough to work against the Neelys."

"Or the Smiths, hmm? Mr. Smith? You're doing that very thing yourself. If you don't want to help her, why didn't you tell your family the truth about this jaunt north? Why are you here?"

He opened his eyes and stared at Munro. "I wanted to take this choice and chance."

"What does that mean?"

Smith didn't answer. He folded his arms tight, hunched his shoulders, closed his eyes, and soon dozed off. He didn't even wake up at station stops. Munro spent most of the journey watching his sleeping companion. He recalled how vulnerable and rather appealing Smith had seemed as he lay in the jail cell. Ha, and that seemed a pale shade to the visceral, gut-deep attraction Munro felt now.

The stubborn chin, the scar at his eye, the firm set of his lips even in sleep, all signs of a roughneck. Munro glared and tried, unsuccessfully, to shift his fascinated attention from Smith. Why the devil did such a creature wake his hunger?

Chapter Nine

The air in Derbyshire seemed thin, and Joshua realized it was because the scents weren't pungent. He found himself drawing in long breaths, trying to get to the bottom of what he was smelling.

Grass. Just a hint of coal smoke, instead of the usual choking drafts of it. Horse manure…and nothing else. It seemed a weak scent. And the sound was muted as well. Once the train went on its way, there were only a few voices and the sound of a single horse's clops and…nothing.

Then they walked off the platform and around the corner, and there was nothing but land stretching out, rolling and empty, like an odd patched quilt of green. It gave him the creeps. He wanted to scurry into the nearest building like a rat escaping to familiar cluttered darkness.

Munro was striding down the dirt road that led away from the little brick stationhouse.

"Where you going?" Smith called.

"The station master said the Jolly Archer is just across the way. You might go around on the street behind High Street and seek out other businesses."

Smith shook off the sense of unreality this place gave him— as much as he could. But he walked and gawped.

The trees took up more space than the buildings and roads. Joshua had to pay some attention to where he walked, but the cleanliness here was absurd. He had to mind the occasional pile of horse dung in the road, but he didn't see or smell a single pile of garbage.

Not what he was used to. When he stepped in a puddle, it almost made him feel better. He saw a woman walking toward him and ducked his head and pretended to read a notice on a church sign. But she was taller and older than Matilda and didn't have a belly either.

She slowed and shot glances at him, as if she'd never seen a stranger before. He tried to look as if he didn't have a care in the world. What did that look like? Hands in pockets, head back, staring into an almost-blue sky. The sun warmed his face.

The woman hurried off. He strolled along. Now that he was on the street, away from those fields, the shop windows looked much like any he knew. It wasn't a foreign land after all. It might just be a very small and tidy corner in London. The lack of people— he could see only three people, all far away—was odd. And the silence unsettled him still. When a bird flew over his head, he could actually hear its wings rustling.

Someone touched his elbow. It was Munro, and he looked pale and upset.

"Come on. We'll go to the other inn now."

"This place has two inns? Did she stay at the other one?"

"Neither. We'll stay the night there. But there's no reason to stay in this town long."

"Why is that?"

"Your wife is gone."

"Do they know where she went?" Then the solemn look on Munro's face made him understand. "Oh." Joshua almost stumbled in shock. Women died having babies every day, but Matilda... It shouldn't matter this much.

"The innkeeper was a gossip, so I have all the details. Mrs. Smith's friend, Mrs. Trout, a reet wealthy fish, as he said, had a family plot where Mrs. Smith is buried," Mr. Munro said softly. "He said the baby survived, and Mrs. Trout's cousin took him in. But then another man spoke up and said the baby didn't live."

"Did she die having it?"

"He thought so. During the birth. He didn't know much but was willing to spill what he had. Apparently, it was all the news here. Another patron there volunteered that her death wasn't to do with the baby. But they agreed that the lady who died was a widow, so she apparently didn't present herself as your wife. You don't need to enter into the picture."

Instead of relief, Joshua felt an unexpected weight in the center of his chest. Responsibility. This was someone he'd given an oath to. He hadn't done such a thing before, except to Big Mervin, but that was an oath given over and over by everyone, a muttered prayer on Sundays.

No one else had given an oath to Matilda Neely. Matilda Smith. During that ceremony, hadn't there been something about protecting her? The fact that it was a sham wedding didn't seem to matter at the moment. Perhaps later it might.

Munro pulled out his watch. "I shall return to the train station. I have to write a telegram to Mr. Kelly."

Joshua followed him in and half listened to the young telegrapher repeat back the short message. *Subject deceased. Details later.*

The operator, a young lady, watched them avidly. The telegram to London wasn't the only news wired around the small town.

"We might return to London," Munro said.

No. Not yet, Joshua wanted to cry out.

"I'd like to see the person who took her in," Joshua said as they emerged from the tiny station.

"Mrs. Trout?"

"Yes. I want to know what actually killed her and the truth of what happened to her baby."

"Let's find a place to stay first. We won't go back to that inn," Munro said. He was the brisk one now. "No need to make ourselves the object of gossip. I'm sure the innkeeper would be glad to tell the lads coming in this evening about how poor Mrs. Smith's family showed up at last."

"Do you suppose your Mr. Kelly will respond soon?"

"Yes. I think he won't be surprised, though."

"What do you mean?"

"I was the only one with a sense of urgency about the search. And I'm the only one hired on to actively search for her, as far as I know. Although I suppose there were those not very subtle watchers hanging about your apartment."

"And if I'm wrong about who your Mr. Kelly's employer…" Joshua fell silent, waiting for Munro to confirm it was Neely, but as usual he didn't.

Should Joshua share what was a family secret and not just his own with a man he didn't know? They'd an attraction to each other, though he'd swear they had more than that. Not trust, not yet, perhaps only shared experiences.

He frowned over at a great huge cow watching him from behind a fence, right on the main street. And this strange place with the wide open spaces. He felt a stranger with only one real companion here: the man with gray eyes that flashed with held-back passion, like no one Joshua had met before.

"Go on," Munro said. He slowed his steps as well.

Joshua almost asked for some coin in exchange for information, an automatic response. But damned if he'd stick with the old pattern of debt and payment. It hadn't done him any good.

And he'd taken an oath to Matilda Neely Smith. He'd find out what had happened to her.

"My father, that is, Big Mervin, thought I'd gotten rid of her. If he thought that, then others will too. And the thing is, the girl was afraid." He rubbed his throat absently. All the talking seemed to make his throat go dry and rough as usual, though the words came smoothly, perhaps because he'd grown used to speaking to Munro. "I thought she was skittish, as who wouldn't be marrying a big stranger of a rival family. But she was terrified beyond that measure."

"Yes, I understood that."

"But it wasn't of me. Or else she wouldn't have left the note. She was afraid of someone else. Her family or mine, I'd suppose. I had no interest in the scheme so I didn't poke around after she left. I think someone else did, though."

"Were you robbed?"

He shook his head. "I went out once or twice during the day, to see if anyone would follow. When I got back, things were shifted. I thought it might have been the maid, hired on by Neely, who came every few days. I didn't pay much attention, but I did think she was not much good at her job."

"Didn't you care?"

"I was waiting to leave the place. It didn't seem to be mine."

"I don't understand. Weren't you a player in the whole thing? Why wouldn't you be interested?"

Joshua shrugged. "I was ready to move back to my old rooms."

"And take up your old life, eh?"

"Maybe. Before." He pointed at his leg. "I just recovered. I'll be a..." He hesitated. "A worker, probably, not heading for the upper ranks." He wondered if that were still true. It seemed as if London and his own life were thousands of miles away. He'd stepped off a cliff when he stepped onto that train, and dropped into something he hadn't even imagined. He'd always suffered from a lack of fancy.

"Did your rise in the Smith family end that night on Chester Street?"

"What do you mean? The injury?"

Munro blinked, then looked away, yet another way he showed discomfort. Joshua had noted that his Mr. Munro had quite a few small but regular sort of tells. Munro said, "Many fathers wouldn't tolerate the disgrace of their sons... That is to say, being discovered at a place like that."

Joshua shrugged. "Big Mervin don't much care about sins as long as they stay hidden. Getting caught was the problem." He thought about the past, before Nick died, before he'd lost interest in the family concern. "Once, yes, I was working my way up. But the business isn't in my blood. And there were plenty of others that burned to be kingpin." He snorted, thinking of the Winters.

"They'd stab their own mum for a few shillings or Big Mervin's approval. Of late, I just wanted to get through the day."

"It must disappoint Big Mervin to have a shirker in his gang. Unwilling to stab his own mum."

"Probably," Joshua said. "My mum's dead, so it won't be put to the test."

"I apologize. That was a poor attempt at humor on my part."

"Was it? Never mind. I rose in Big Mervin's books when I got rid of my wife along with the evidence linking me to her disappearance."

A look of horror flitted across Munro's face.

Joshua said, "That's what he thinks, not what happened. Is that what you believe I did?"

"No."

Munro said it with such emphasis, Joshua felt warmed. Had he earned his trust?

Then Munro explained. "From what I saw on the train today, I believe you're not used to travel. You hadn't left London recently. If we agree that Mrs. Smith died here, then you were not responsible for her death."

"Mrs. Smith? Ha." Joshua wanted Munro to have faith in him. Pushing the sensible argument went right up against that, but he didn't stop himself. "You didn't believe me when I first gave you the name Smith. The woman who died here might have been another person who wanted to hide her real name and not my wife."

Munro gave him a look he knew, a brow and corner of mouth quirked. Amusement or disgust. "The innkeeper confirmed that Mrs. Smith arrived about the time she sent the letter to you. And a female with a baby on the way, in this backwater? Until I find evidence otherwise, I won't question the identity of the late Mrs. Joshua Smith."

"Odd to hear my name with hers," Joshua muttered.

"Yes, I expect it would be. You were joined in marriage, and almost at once, your wife fled your nuptial bower."

"She'd no reason to fear me."

Munro's eyebrow rose, and his half smile seemed to turn thoughtful. "So perhaps it truly was your family that she feared?"

"That." Joshua nodded. "Neely didn't seem to care. Didn't even come to her wedding. But yes, the families of Neely and Smith weren't always on the friendliest of terms."

"Was Neely expanding his territory as well?"

Joshua shrugged. He'd heard rumors that Neely wanted to play a big game or two, of course, but wasn't sure it was anyone's business, not even this interesting ex-copper.

"We already know the Smiths want to go where the real money lay." Munro's sidelong look at him was obvious.

"Don't know what you mean."

"Of course you do. Picking pockets is all very well, but one gains so much more if one extracts the cash from the banks directly."

Damn. Joshua had said as much himself. He looked around for another topic and caught sight of a stone house with a placard on a pole in the front garden. From a distance, the faded painting on the sign seemed to be a large white dog. "That's where we're heading, isn't it?"

Munro gave a disgusted snort of laughter. "Yes, but you're not escaping this conversation."

"No?" Joshua walked through the narrow gap in the stone fence surrounding the house. So much gray stone. The dog on the placard turned out to be a goat standing on some grapes.

"I need to understand all the circumstances if we're to discover why Mrs. Smith ran off," Munro said in a voice as soft as Joshua's. "What had she to fear in your family or hers. I think you trust me more than you did and are ready to tell me what you know. But fine, I'll allow you to put me off for the moment. We'll get rooms, wash, and then meet to talk more."

They walked through a vestibule and into a windowless, empty room with painted hands on signs pointing at doors indicating the publican, the private parlor, and the ladies parlor. The space was small and cluttered. Once Joshua's eyes adjusted to the dark, he could see it was tidy enough, with no dust and the pleasant, chilly scent of beer and wood-smoke.

"You're paying," Joshua reminded him.

"Yes, indeed."

Joshua attempted the best imitation of a gentleman he could, rolling his R's. "Then I require a room with a private parlor and the best view. Certainly not overlooking the stable."

Munro's laugh was genuine this time. "Where'd you learn to speak like that, Mr. Smith? Your brother?"

Joshua didn't answer. Of course it had been Nick.

The innkeeper came in, then, shrugging on a coat over his bare sleeves and apron. He had a nearly bald head, with a fringe of gray hair around the back of his head. His pointed nose and chin reminded Joshua of Punch, of Punch and Judy.

When the innkeeper smiled, he showed such white straight teeth, they had to be false. "Sirs. How'd ye do? We aren't serving food at the moment. Come back in two hours for dinner. Lamb, I promise, and not mutton."

"I'm not certain about that, but we'd like two rooms for the night."

The innkeeper furrowed his gray brows as if concentrating on weighty matters. "I got two in a pinch, but there's just the one suitable for guests."

"Both will do." Munro's back straightened. He didn't glance in Joshua's direction.

The innkeeper rubbed his jaw. "The two rooms is attached. To be honest, the one is just a storeroom. But I could shift some furniture and whatnot..." He paused and stared up at the ceiling. "Although I 'spect it'll take a while."

He so clearly wished they'd just request the single room, Joshua wanted to laugh.

"Both rooms, please," Munro said.

The innkeeper slumped a little. "I'll have to charge a full rate, you see, though it's but a small room with no—"

"Both rooms," Munro repeated firmly. He didn't need to be so obvious that he'd do anything not to sleep near Joshua. On the other hand, it was good to have that sort of power. Joshua wasn't a bully, but he liked unsettling Mr. Munro, probably because the man did the same to him simply by breathing, walking, talking, looking at him, as he did now, the brow up.

Joshua poked him in the ribs. "I don't mind one."

Munro didn't have that half smile; his mouth was a thin line of annoyance. He turned away from Joshua, picked up a pen, and wrote in the book the innkeeper pushed at him.

"Come, then, gentlemen." The innkeeper trotted up the stairs without looking back to make sure they followed.

A vase of silk flowers at the top of the steps was dusty, but otherwise, the inn seemed as well-kept as any place Joshua had ever been.

The keeper led them to a room that was surprisingly large and sunny, though the ceiling was pitched because it was under the eaves. A four-poster stood in the middle of the floor, with a yellow cover and matching yellow rug.

"Here's the other room." The innkeeper pushed open a door. There were indeed crates with excelsior falling out. The piles of chairs took up most of the space, some on top of the bed. "I'll send along the lad to straighten the room right away."

"Yes," Munro said. "As soon as possible."

The innkeeper handed them a key, then left the room. Munro stood in the doorway and fingered his chin.

"I forgot to ask for hot water to be sent up," he said. "I'll go directly."

The nervous fellow was out the bedroom door before Joshua could say a thing. With a sigh, Joshua put his satchel on the bed to make it clear he marked his territory, then explored the room. That took less than a minute since the bureau, writing desk, and clothes press were all empty, except for a lump of melted wax on the writing desk. He stretched out on the bed, his boots on the satchel, his hands behind his head as he tried to imagine sharing the bed with Munro.

A few minutes later, a parade of people entered the room: a maid with a water pitcher, the lad with a bucket, and Munro bringing up the rear.

The boy went into the box room, and a few moments later, there was clunking and thumping. The maid put the pitcher on the washstand, then went to the fireplace to build up a fire.

Joshua sat up. "The day's too warm for a fire, isn't it?"

"You never know," Munro said. Clearly, Munro wanted to avoid being alone in this bedroom with Joshua.

"I'll go exploring." Joshua swung his feet down, then rose from the bed.

"Give me a minute, and I'll join you downstairs," Munro said.

Joshua walked down the stairs, thinking of how they each had their bugaboos they shied away from. He avoided talking about Big Mervin, and Munro tried to pretend to feel normal in Joshua's presence. Maybe he could get Munro to work on making an exchange. *Admit you want to kiss me, and I'll tell you about the job Big Mervin planned for a bank.*

A few minutes later, Munro joined him, and they set off, Munro immediately going at a brisk pace.

He looked over his shoulder at Joshua. "We want to look as if we know where we're going."

"Why? Everyone knows everyone else in this place. We'll be marked as strangers. Where are we going?"

"To visit the widow."

"Who?"

"The innkeeper said this was the lady who cared for and then buried your wife. She is not far, less than three miles down this road."

Joshua furtively rubbed his leg and hurried to catch up.

The few houses of High Street gave way to another stretch of greenery that seemed to go on forever. He'd seen such green from the train, but the smoke-smeared glass hadn't shown him the vivid color, and when he'd tried to lower the window in the car, it had jammed. He stared at the green until his eyes hurt. The occasional patch of trees, gray rock walls, and tall hedgerows were practically the only things interrupting all the rolling velvet fields.

It made him feel too open, as if a giant creature from above could swoop down and carry them off. "We should turn back," he said.

"Not on your life. We have come this far and I need to understand why the stories we've heard are inconsistent." Munro gave him a curious glance. "We might find out the truth. You insisted you wanted to know. What has changed?"

"Nothing. Let's keep walking." He didn't have a good answer other than the dizziness caused by so much open space.

When had he become so cowardly? The train and now this. No. He would not allow fear to rule his actions.

To distract himself, he asked, "What do you know of the place we're visiting?"

"The lady is wealthy. She moved here from London with her late husband, who was many years older than she."

"How did you learn that much in such a short time?"

"A very bored innkeeper during a quiet time of the day in a small town is an excellent source of information." He pointed to a hill beyond a copse of trees. "I think that's her property."

"Did he say anything else about the widow?"

"Mrs. Trout is considered a local beauty. Other than that, no."

"I didn't hear that name wrong before. Trout? Like a fish?"

"Exactly."

"Wonder what her maiden name was. Matilda must've met her in London," Joshua said.

The road became dirt again, easier on his leg, but he slowed his step anyway. Now that they were well past most of the houses of the village, surely no one watched.

"I believe they met in the city, yes. And that likely means that Mrs. Trout is not well-bred. I don't know the details of Miss Neely's education, but I doubt she had a governess or was sent to finishing school, so the two girls likely met in the same sort of world you occupied."

"You calling me ill-bred?" Joshua said with mock horror.

Munro's mouth twitched. "Yes, I suppose I am. My own background is hardly Eton or Harrow."

"You forget I saw your house, Mr. Munro. Even a scuttler such as myself knows that's a gent's establishment."

"That house belonged to my mother's family, and I had nothing to do with them until I was full-grown."

"How did you come by the plummy accent?"

"I was sent to a boarding school in England by my maternal grandfather. My father's family is poor."

"No sin in that," Joshua said.

107

Munro gave him a surprised glance. "No, none at all. Though we stopped seeing eye-to-eye when I understood that they were proud of their lack of education and hatred of outsiders. If my mother and her father hadn't insisted I get an education in England, I would've eventually ended up in Perth. I'd likely still be fishing with my father."

"You'd talk even funnier than you do now."

"No doubt about that." Munro sounded distracted. He walked faster.

Joshua sped up as well, happy to realize that all the walking made his leg hurt less, not more. "You don't get along with them now? Your father's family?"

"We rub along well enough as long as I remember to keep my mouth closed. And to stop talking like an English toff." He glanced at Joshua, his brows furrowed. "I imagine you get that as well, since you don't sound like an East Ender."

Joshua rubbed two fingers over his throat. "I barely sound like a person."

"I meant your accent isn't cockney."

"Oh. That. I told you why."

"Tell me how, then."

"Big Mervin hired a former instructor, a brandy shunter, to tutor Nick, who taught me."

"The tutor was a drunkard?" Munro said.

"Isn't that what I said?"

They came around a bend in the woods, and ahead of them lay a neat stone fence at least six feet tall with a large iron gate facing the road. Joshua gave a whistle. "Now that's something grand."

"Indeed it is." Munro sniffed. "I'd thought the innkeeper was exaggerating or didn't know the true meaning of 'wealthy,' but this is impressive."

Chapter Ten

Munro stopped by the iron double gate and called out, "Hey there, open up."

A little man came from the house next to it. "What do you think you want?"

"My name is Munro, and I'm here to speak to Mrs. Trout."

"Got an appointment?" The old man wore a bulky black jacket, and Munro realized he wasn't fat but wore several jumpers under the black wool.

"No, but I've come all the way from London. I wish to talk to her about her late friend, Mrs. Smith."

"Another one," said the man in disgust. "You'd be the second in two days."

"Oh?" Munro blinked. "Can you tell me about the other man?"

"I could, but don't see why I should."

Munro stifled a sigh and pulled some coins from his pocket. "Will a shilling give me a description?"

The gatekeeper reached a gnarled hand between the iron bars. He took the coins, counted, and pocketed them before answering. "The one said he was a policeman. But he cut up rough when I said I wouldn't let him in unless he talked to our Constable Weaver, and then he stormed off and didn't come back. I had the boy fetch the constable to see if the so-called policeman had checked in with him."

"He hadn't," Munro guessed.

The man touched the side of his nose. "Precisely."

"If I have a word with the local law enforcement and he accompanied me, would you let me in?"

"Maybe."

"First allow me to pass along a message." Munro pulled a leather-bound pad from his inside pocket along with the stub of a pencil.

"You are a cop for certain," Smith muttered. "Carrying the occurrence book everywhere you go."

Munro ignored him as he scribbled a note to Mrs. Trout. He didn't say who'd hired him, only that he was investigating on behalf of a party who'd sounded an alarm about Mrs. Smith, and now hoped to gather details of her death.

"Ask if we can visit Matilda's grave," Smith said, surprising him again.

He nodded and added that line. He also added his whole name, Sir Ross Eden Munro.

A sharp breeze swept past them as they walked up the drive and clouds began to crowd the blue sky.

"Just as changeable weather here as in London," Smith said.

"We're on the same continent, not even hundreds of miles away."

Smith turned and looked behind them, down the hill to the copse of trees beyond the big iron gate. "Feels like a different world."

A footman appeared at the front steps, dressed in livery that was years out of date—wig, breeches, stockings, and all. Smith gave a small snort. "Looks like the people who live here aren't much like Londoners either."

The footman led them toward a drawing room, where a young lady stood at the door, watching them walk down the corridor toward her. Hardly the habit of the wealthy young women Munro knew, but otherwise, she looked the part.

He didn't know ladies' fashion, but she appeared neat and respectable in a lavender gown with black lace at the neck and sleeves. Mourning, he supposed. Well-tailored and expensive cloth. With pale skin, pink cheeks and lips, dark hair and eyes, the young lady was also entirely lovely. "Snow White," Munro said.

"What?"

"The fairy tale?"

Smith shrugged. Munro wanted to demand if he knew any tales, but now they were too close to their hostess to say more.

She gave a regal nod. "Sir Ross."

Smith started. He whispered, "Who's that? You, Munro?"

Munro ignored him and bowed to the lady. "Good day, Mrs. Trout."

Smith grumbled quietly, probably a curse.

Mrs. Trout's smooth forehead puckered with the hint of a frown. "I pride myself on my knowledge of titles, even of baronets. But I don't recall the name Munro."

"I inherited the title from my maternal grandfather. My father is still alive."

"For that transference of the baronetcy, your family must have had a special remainder, then. Ah." She walked into the room, small graceful steps, over to a large volume sitting on a stand, and leafed through it. "I see. Ah, yes. Your grandfather must have been William Eden. He has passed, and now the son of Adair Munro is the baronet. And here you are, Sir Ross. Sounds like the wind blowing dried autumn leaves. Sir Ross."

Smith gave a snort of laughter.

Mrs. Trout gave Smith a quick, cold look up and down. Her examination stopped at the scar on his cheek. "Will you introduce me to your companion, Sir Ross?"

"This is Mr. Joshua. He is aiding me in my inquiries."

Smith, who'd balked and mumbled at Munro's name, didn't so much as blink at the transformation of his own name. He did a sort of head bob and bow. "Ma'am," he said. Not elegant, but not bad.

The door opened, and Mrs. Trout's chin rose. "Here is my sister-in-law, Miss Aurelia Trout."

A large woman of about fifty bustled into the room. She gave them a vague smile, then, without a word, went to a seat next to the empty fireplace. She picked up a pile of yarn and needles and began working.

"Good morning, Miss Trout," Munro said.

She nodded but didn't look up from the gray wool in her lap.

"One must make apologies for Miss Trout." Mrs. Trout whispered the words. "She is uninterested in social activity. She understands that she must come when I entertain company, but otherwise has little interest in the matter."

"You are most kind to give her a home," Munro said.

It proved the wrong tactic. Mrs. Trout turned into a frost queen at once. Her cheeks grew even redder. "This was Aurelia's home for all her life before I met Geoffrey. The fact of the matter is she was most kind in accepting me as her brother's bride." She squeezed her hands tight and straightened her shoulders. "I beg your pardon. One doesn't wish to fly off the handle at commonplace remarks."

"Not at all," Munro said, intrigued. Her high-strung manner might be normal or it might be nervousness. He'd have to prod a bit more.

With a graceful sweep of her hand, she indicated two chairs and a sofa. After an awkward pause while the three of them remained standing looking at each other, she took a seat on a hard-backed chair and carefully folded her hands in her lap.

Smith carefully lowered himself to a rickety chair next to her, and Munro took the sofa across from them.

She raised a small, pale hand as if to halt questions before they started. "There is very little I can tell you about my unfortunate visitor, but one understands that you must ask." Before Munro could reply, she went on. "You expressed a desire to visit her grave? Might I ask why? I assure you there is nothing to see. She is indeed buried. We just last week placed a stone, though it has her name and nothing else. I was unsure of her birthdate, you see."

Definitely nervous. And despite her impeccable accent and her grace, there was something just a little strange about Mrs. Trout.

She shifted in her chair, smoothed her gown over her lap, and cleared her throat. "I beg your pardon. One finds the entire episode most upsetting and I... One cannot understand why no one came earlier looking for the poor dear girl. The only *person*"—her emphasis made the word sound like a vile insult—"was a vulgar creature come yesterday. Mr. Reed, the butler, believes that person was from London and was up to no good. One cannot imagine what the fellow wanted, nor does one care to find out. The poor lady and her child are in a better place now."

"I have heard various stories, including a version in which the child survived."

"Indeed? Did you hear that in the village?"

He nodded.

"One does abhor gossip. She survived for a time, but alas, no, the poor darling baby girl soon joined her mother in heaven."

A girl? The innkeeper had said it was a boy. Maybe he wasn't a good source of information after all. Munro said, "That must have been terribly upsetting to lose your friend like that."

"Ah, as to that. I really didn't know the woman, you see."

Smith made a small *hmm* and shifted in his chair. His brows rose, and he looked at Munro, who got his message and asked, "How did she come into your care, then?"

She gazed into the air in front of herself as if watching a heartrending scene that the other two couldn't see. "I was shopping in the village with Miss Trout, and a sudden rain shower started up. We couldn't very well go into the Jolly Archer, two ladies on their own, so we hurried into the train station, where we found the lady in question looking very poorly and, ah, very, very close to her time."

She seemed to lose her place in the recital and cleared her throat again. "Naturally, we couldn't leave her there. We helped her to the dog cart and brought her straight back here. She fell ill that night and…" Mrs. Trout shook her head. Her lip trembled, her nose became a delicate pink, and a single tear dropped from her large dark eye and trickled down her cheek. She raised her hands and gave a single broken sob into her palms. "So very tragic. Ah, the poor darling girl."

"Ah," Smith said. "Ha."

She pulled a lacy handkerchief from her pocket, dabbed at her eyes and her nose, and ignored him.

Smith grinned at her. "I think I got it now. Were you at Picton's? I been there more'n once."

Her hand froze for less than a second. She refolded the handkerchief and tucked it back away. "Mr. Joshua? Are you feeling quite the thing?" She gave him a puzzled smile, showing a dimple. "Should I ring for some tea? Or perhaps you'd prefer something stronger?"

Tapping his chin thoughtfully with two blunt fingers, he leaned forward and stared at her. "No, that was not you." His fingers stilled, and a slow smile spread over his face. "Ah. Now I remember, it was the musical number after the tableaux. Ahh. Yes."

She was about to speak again, but Smith cut her off.

"Mind you, the establishment is far too fancy for a bloke like me, but during a flush time, some of us went to the Alhambra." He gave a little cough, then croaked out a song. "'*Ah, she said, Ah, let me hear your sorrow, vast and wide and deep. Ah, he replied, let me hear your joy, so you my heart can keep.*' Or some bilge like that. The Ah Song. You had a very nice voice." He smiled and rested his elbows on his knees, nothing like a gentleman. "Better than the song."

"Mr. Joshua. I believe that you—"

Smith snapped his fingers. "You're that girl. That's a fact. But here's my guess? Trout was a stage-door johnny."

Munro wondered if he should step in—this was his investigation, after all—but Smith was doing a fine job without any help.

Munro couldn't resist asking, "Do you suppose that's a story bruited about the area? We might explore that possibility at the Jolly Archer, have a talk with the chatty innkeeper."

Mrs. Trout closed her eyes, heaved a sigh, opened them again, then daintily twisted in her chair to look at Munro. She held her hands out, palms up to him, pleading. "Blackmail, gentlemen? Sad that you'd stoop so low. There is no need for this nonsense to be broadcast about the village. You came to me to talk about my poor visitor, did you not? Surely the police have no interest in unrelated matters."

"As to that, my note did mention that I worked at the London Metropolitan. But I don't any longer."

She rose to her feet, fast but graceful. "Then I demand that you go at once. I am perfectly willing to talk to the proper authorities about my late visitor, but not to someone walking in off the street. This is outrageous."

"I have the authority of her family to discover her whereabouts."

The pink-cheeked lady went pale. "Her-her family? Who? What?"

"Her family," he said again. "But see here, Mrs. Trout, that upset you. I want to know what you think. If you have some reason they shouldn't know about her fate, tell me. That's not a challenge. It's an honest question."

She glanced at her sister-in-law, then said in a low voice, "They didn't deserve her. Her father was a villain who allowed unspeakable things to happen to her and then married her off to some oaf to gain information and a foothold in a competitor's family."

Smith didn't so much as twitch. He was a far better actor than the lady in front of them.

"Then my associate, Mr. ah, Joshua, was correct?" Damn that *ah* of hers was contagious.

"Of what are you speaking?" She raised her already arched eyebrows.

"You were an actress at the Alhambra, and that was where you met your husband-to-be."

"That's nothing to do with you." Her perfect accent slipped, and a bit of London's less well-bred came into her voice.

"Where did you meet Miss Neely? In London?"

"Why are you asking these stupid questions? I did not hurt the lady. I only helped her. And if it comes to that, if her family wishes to know how she lived and died, they should come apply to me themselves. I expected the police, you know."

"You met her in London, and you were her friend," Smith said, his low voice ominous. "She trusted you. She fled to you. And now she's dead."

She seemed to slump, but only for a second. "I met her in London in a hat shop. There. Are you satisfied? Is that enough information? I met her, we shared an interest in millinery and…and in laughter. Then I met my dear Mr. Trout. I left that horrible place and have been happy ever since. At least until my poor friend came to me." She hastily added, "Ah and yes, of course I was not happy when I lost Mr. Trout. He taught me to appreciate the real value in the world." Her gaze drifted to the big copy of Debretts.

She leaned back in the chair. "I told you that story about not knowing her because I don't care for any part of my past to visit me here, other than my dear friend. I was horrified to see her, but only because she'd come to a terrible pass. Matilda Neely deserved better than...than ravishment and a brutish husband."

Munro had to ask the question. He carefully did not allow his eyes to drift in Smith's direction. "Did her husband rape her?"

"I-I don't think so. By the time she wed, she'd had more than enough of that sort of man and kept herself safe. But he would have. From what she said, he was huge and callous. He had a limp, a scar, and a terrible voi—" She stopped speaking. Her eyes grew large.

She leaned forward, grabbed the bell, and rang it hard.

Almost at once, two footmen, who'd clearly been waiting just outside the room, burst through the doors. Their grand entrance was nothing like a normal servant's arrival. Even Miss Trout looked up from her gray wool.

Mrs. Trout was on her feet, and so Munro also stood. She pointed a trembling finger at Smith and Munro. "These men are going to leave now. They are not welcome back."

Smith still sat, his bad leg stretched out in front of himself. "Yeah. I'm Mrs. Smith's husband." He actually smiled at Mrs. Trout. "It's fine, though. She wrote me. Told me where she was. Told me you was her friend. That's why I knew. See, ma'am? She didn't hate me or she wouldn't have written. I don't know what happened after she left, but I do know that."

Munro hadn't seen the missive from Mrs. Smith, but he knew there was no mention of names. Smith had been honestly amused by Mrs. Trout's name. Munro made a mental note that Smith did a good job of lying or exaggeration. Good to know.

Mrs. Trout raised that dainty hand chest high, arm straight to signal a halt to the footmen without looking at them. Such a music hall motion, Munro wondered why he hadn't seen it right away.

The footmen stopped immediately.

Without lowering her arm, Mrs. Trout said, "I shall give you five more minutes, Mr. Smith. Then you will leave and never darken my doors again. Stephen, please tell Mr. Reed to give those instructions to all the staff."

"Reed's your butler?" Smith asked. "How is it he didn't answer the door?"

"Not that it is any of your concern, but I believe he is in the village on an errand."

The footmen retreated, and Munro and Mrs. Trout resumed their seats.

Smith pulled in a long breath. "What you said about that wedding. Yes. I didn't know and didn't care about the arrangement between our fathers before it, but I knew there was a deal. Always is with us. She tell you that?"

Mrs. Trout nodded. "To be seen as nothing more than an object to be bought or sold..." Her lips trembled again. "It's something we spoke of and knew."

Smith rubbed his chin with his thumb, and the soft rasp of his whiskers nearly covered his next words. "I'm sorry."

Munro wondered what his apology meant, but he had no time if he took Mrs. Trout's threat of five minutes seriously. He needed to get as much information as possible. "Do you know of anyone else she contacted, other than Mr. Smith?"

"I didn't know she'd written to him. I don't check all the correspondence going out of this house."

"Wouldn't the butler?"

Before answering, she looked at Miss Trout, who gave a small nod. Apparently Mrs. Trout still didn't know all the ins and outs of wealthy households. "Perhaps," she said. "But I doubt he'd recall every single piece of post."

"You expected a visit from the police? Did she contact the London authorities?"

She raised her shoulders in an extravagant shrug. "As I made clear, I don't know whom she contacted."

"Did she express any specific reason she had to flee London?"

"Ah. Alas, no."

He wondered if there was a direct correlation between the word "Ah" and a lie coming from her lips.

"Do you have any guesses?"

"I already told you," she snapped. "Her father, her family, was horrible." She glanced at Smith.

"Did she leave anything behind?"

"She came with the clothes on her back and nothing else. It weren't—wasn't a lie about her state when we met in the station. It was also pouring down rain that day. You might ask Miss Trout if you don't believe me." She seemed to be growing more, not less, belligerent as they spoke.

"She wrote a note to me, and she mentioned taking jewelry," Smith said. "I had none for her to steal. So…" He tilted his head to the side, inviting her comment.

"Oh? There is nothing I know of." Her face had grown red. Barely suppressed anger or embarrassment? "Perhaps that is how she purchased her train ticket? We never discussed the matter."

She reached for the bell again.

"Beg pardon, but you did promise us five minutes, Mrs. Trout."

She gave an unladylike growl—but folded her arms without ringing the bell.

"Did the local doctor give a cause for her death?" Munro asked.

"Child fever. You might look at the death record if you don't believe me."

"One was filed?"

"Of course."

"Do you know the name of the attending doctor?"

"We had a midwife. A very pleasant lady by the name of Mrs. Griggs, who lives just south of our estate." She'd regained her calm and looked almost bored again. "It was not Mrs. Griggs's fault that dear Matilda succumbed several days after the birth."

Munro's investigative instincts prickled. "I thought it was almost immediately."

"Days," she said firmly. "Now I will ask one of the footmen to lead you to the gravesite for you to pay your respects. And if you require anything else to prove to Matilda's family that she has indeed gone to a better place, let me know. I'd rather not be in communication with them, but perhaps we might arrange for a photograph to be taken of her tombstone."

She stood and walked to the sitting room door with them. "Please do not return. If you require more information, you may send a note of inquiry. I shall not be home to you if you return. Stephen, please escort these men to see Mrs. Smith's grave, then make sure they leave."

The footman guided them down the hall and out the door without a single word.

Still silent, he walked down the steps, along the gravel drive to a small path leading away. Smith and Munro dropped back a few paces so they could talk.

"He's dressed funny," Smith muttered.

"It's the traditional garb for a footman. You've never seen one?"

Smith shook his head.

"The strange thing about those footmen are how large they are and how fast they are to respond to the bell. I think the household has been put into some sort of alert. Any visitors inquiring about Mrs. Smith in any way are cause for fear."

"Yes," Smith said. "Or should I say 'ah, indeed.'"

His imitation of Mrs. Trout made Munro laugh.

Mrs. Smith's grave lay in the family cemetery on the far edge of the estate. Most of the headstones were quite old—Mrs. Smith's and Mr. Trout's graves were the only ones from the last decade.

Smith stood near the tombstone for a long minute, then slowly got to his knees by the rather plain granite stone. Munro glanced over at the footman, who stared at them with a scowl as if they'd whipped out their todgers and were pissing on the grave.

Munro walked over to join Smith. He knelt next to him, wanting to comfort the man but entirely unsure how to do such a thing. Remaining silent seemed better than *Deepest condolences on the death of the wife I thought you hardly knew.*

Smith ran his hand over the dirt, which was still fresh. He glanced up at the footman, who'd walked away to examine an angel perched over a long-departed Trout's grave. Smith said something quiet.

"I beg your pardon?" Munro asked.

"There's still something slippery about Mrs. Trout."

Munro drew in a long breath of relief. He'd almost pulled Smith into a soothing embrace. Thank goodness he hadn't. He said, "Very funny."

A grin flashed across Smith's face. He grew serious again. "You're right that the whole household is afraid. But not of the law. She didn't try to throw you out when she thought you were a cop."

"I think she's a snob, and she didn't throw me out because of my baronetcy."

"Maybe." Smith rose, carefully balanced on one leg, but he didn't wobble.

Munro tried not to stare at the smooth power of that motion.

Smith asked, "You being Sir Ross another reason why you left the force?"

"In part, yes."

"Why didn't you tell me?"

"It hardly seemed relevant, and don't forget that most of our interactions have been adversarial."

"That so?"

Smith was examining him sideways, that knowing smirk on his face. The footman ambled in their direction.

Munro raised an imperious hand. "A minute longer, please."

"Still got the policeman's touch," Smith murmured. "He froze like a statue."

"Whatever the truth about Mrs. Smith, she obviously shared her fears with Mrs. Trout. The lady is skittish, especially for a female used to a less refined world in London."

"She might always be high-strung. Actress."

Munro sighed. "Perhaps. The sister-in-law is another strange one."

Smith gave one of his huffs that sounded like a half laugh. "I half thought she could be Matilda, but she looks nothing like her."

"Yes, she looks years older than Mrs. Smith, although if they are actresses, they could perhaps be geniuses with face paint?"

Smith's eyes narrowed as if he were examining a faraway scene. He shook his head. "Matilda was far thinner and smaller, except for her belly. You can add padding, but not all over. And I think Miss Trout's taller as well."

The footman moved to another grave. Smith watched him, then asked Munro, "Should we go?"

"I'd like to wait until our friend over there is positively impatient and ready to flee. He'd answer questions just to get rid of us."

Smith inspected the footman, who now stood, back to them, again shuffling from foot to foot as if he required the necessary. "More like he'll just give us a swift kick in the arse."

Munro murmured, "I would like to see him try—with you, at any rate."

Smith's laugh was real.

A soft rain began to fall. "This will help," Munro said.

"Ugh." Smith pulled up the collar of his jacket.

"Stay here and look mournful," Munro ordered.

He walked over the soft loam and grass to the footman. "Your name is Stephen?"

The footman must have been lost in thought, for he looked up sharply and took a step backward. "Yes, sir."

"Have you been in service long?"

The footman shuffled from foot to foot. "No. Worked for the butcher till recently."

"How recently?"

"Not long ago." The footman inched toward the path back to the gravel drive. "Shall I show you the way to the gate?"

"Not yet." Munro waved in Smith's direction. "I shall encourage him to give up his vigil. But first I wonder could you tell us about the other person who came to enquire about the late Mrs. Smith?"

The footman wiped a dribble of water from his forehead and hunched over. "He didn't get past the gate, so no, sir."

"No description?"

The rain fell harder, pattering on their hats and on the leaves of the trees.

Stephen gave an impatient stamp of his feet in their leather shoes with gold buckles. "I heard a bit, yes. From Summers, in town, I mean."

"And?"

"Boys at the Archer said he's a bandy-legged fellow with an accent from London. A short fellow with red muttonchops and several missing teeth. That's right, and he had a squint. Sir, might we not get out of this rain? Looks like it might turn into a downpour."

"I wonder if you can tell me about the lady who died."

The footman wiped his face again, then folded his arms. "I can't tell you a thing."

"Do you like your employer?"

"Sir." He scowled. "I don't think that's right. Not at all."

That much protest gave an answer to a question Munro hadn't asked. And of course Mrs. Trout was an attractive young lady.

Munro shook his head and suppressed a smile. "No, I simply meant do you trust her and feel she is an honest person?"

The footman reddened. "Yes, sir. Of course. We must take cover from this storm or risk catching a chill."

"We're strong, healthy men. We can take a bit of weather."

The footman gave a loud sniff.

"Only a few more questions."

Stephen folded his arms. "Well?" He didn't bother with the "sir" anymore.

"Are there other newcomers to the village?"

"We get artists and so on." He jutted his chin in the direction of some trees. "They like them hills. I don't take a count of all that get off the train. Best to speak to the innkeepers."

He wasn't as useful as Munro had hoped. With some difficulty, Munro shoved his wet hands into his pockets to gather up a sizeable tip, nearly a pound, which he handed over.

"I'm willing to pay for any information relating to the young lady who got off the train and ended up in this household."

Stephen pocketed the coins, then flicked some water off his forehead and muttered something about his job. His horsehair wig was losing its shape, and Munro took pity on him and on Smith, whose cheeks had gone very pink with the chill.

"We'll go now. And Stephen, I'll tell no one about any information you gave me, but do feel free to spread word of my interest. You or any other interested parties will find me at the Goat and Grapes for tonight. What's more, if anyone else from the household comes to visit me there, I shall make sure to reward you as well."

The footman merely stared at him.

"Come on," Munro called to Smith.

The rain died away almost entirely as they followed the footman to the wide iron gates of the house, where they waited without speaking for the gatekeeper to hurry out of the little stone house and unlock the gates. Munro considered asking the gatekeeper to confirm the description of the stranger that Stephen had given him, but the footman still hung about waiting for them to go. It would destroy the small amount of trust Munro had built with him.

"Seems funny to keep these giant gates locked in the middle of the day in the middle of the country," Munro remarked in a loud voice. "Are you expecting an invading army?"

No one answered.

As he walked away from the sprawling grounds, Munro looked over his shoulder several times. Until he and Smith had rounded a corner that brought them out of sight, the footman and gatekeeper stood on the other side of the locked gate and watched them trudge away.

Chapter Eleven

Joshua pulled off his hat and shook off the water. A fine drizzle still fell, but he didn't mind. Rain in the country seemed exotic, almost wild, compared to London storms. Sometimes, discomfort made him feel more interested in the world. He almost said as much to Munro, but decided that seemed too intimate and peculiar.

"You didn't get anything from the servant?" he asked.

"Nothing worth making us so wet. We can keep a lookout for a bandy-legged Londoner with missing teeth and red hair. And muttonchops. He's our policeman, well, a sham policeman, since it doesn't sound as if he would fit the height requirement."

Smith slowed. "A short bloke?"

"Yes. Do you know him?"

"Maybe one of the men hanging about my apartment. If he's the same, I'll wager he's a Neely man." Joshua pulled out a handkerchief and wiped his face as they walked. "He lives on the ground floor—or his friends do. Below the apartment Neely gave me and his daughter. I passed him in the corridor. More than once."

"We'll look for him," Munro declared.

"I will. You just told Stephen you'd be hanging about the Goat and Grapes waiting for information. I'll tramp around, keeping my eyes open and scaring the housewives. Easily spooked bunch in this place."

He must have sounded annoyed, because Munro challenged him. "You wanted to get out of London, didn't you?"

"I left because of the Winters."

A lie of course. He'd left London and trailed after Munro because he wanted him. Letting the man slip out of his life had seemed like tossing a pouch of gold pieces into the middle of the Thames—a shame and a waste. That awkward truth made him want to change the subject. "Best I go on the hunt. I'll know the little man from London. You won't."

"Yes, that's a good point. We shall stop at the Jolly Archer first," Munro said.

Still nettled by the realization that he'd tagged along with Munro mostly because of desire, Joshua asked, "You don't trust me to find the man on my own?"

Munro only shrugged, which stung more than it should have.

Joshua growled. "I know it's been the longest sort of day, but I have saved your life at least twice today. I've come haring off up north because of you." He hurriedly added, "To help you. Find my wife. And now I've learned she's dead." That did explain some of his bad mood. Hearing of the plucky girl's death had given him the pip.

Munro made a soft humming sound.

"What?" Joshua demanded.

"Have you noticed how odd her end seems? That is to say, the story of her passing changes depending upon whom you ask. That tells me someone's changing the facts for some reason. That could be a sign she faced some sort of danger, and, if it came from London, you might be under the same threat as well."

That hadn't occurred to him, and the thought didn't bother him much, at least when it came to his own safety. He was always on the alert for danger at home.

The breeze picked up, and clouds scuttered across the late-afternoon sky. This place seemed to hold a menace of silence. It pressed in on a man, more unsettling than shouted threats.

They walked quickly enough that his rain-dampened clothing didn't chill Joshua, though the wet socks in his boots chaffed his feet.

The Jolly Archer was far larger than the Goat and Grapes. They glanced into the salon bar, but rejected the more comfortable carpeted area for the public tap room with its bare wood floors and wooden furniture.

A number of bearded men with boots and rough tweed clothing stood near the fire, chatting.

"Farmers, you suppose?" Joshua asked.

Munro shook his head. "Their accent is too well-educated. I expect they're the artists and fishermen the footman mentioned. I'm going to go talk to the innkeeper again. He'll remember my tip. You go ahead and make an order for food as well as a pint for me and whatever you want to drink. We've earned it all."

"What do you eat?"

Munro hunted through his pockets without looking up. "Anything other than oatmeal. I can't abide the stuff. Ah. Here we go." He pulled out his notebook and pencil again. "Still dry, thank goodness. Righty-ho. I'll be back soon."

He walked out the door at the back of the room, leaving Joshua to make his way to a table. He picked one at the far end of the room, away from the other customers.

The men in the room watched him, perhaps wondering if they should include him in the general conversation. He gave them a Big Mervin glare. He must have mastered his father's scowl, because their attention hurriedly shifted away from him. Munro was the one of them trained in the art of wringing information from people, so he could indulge in all the pleasant talk.

Joshua gave an order for stew and ale, then pulled a rickety chair up to the table. He wished he could sit closer to the fire now that the day had turned cold and he was still wet.

One of the men in the room, yet another large man in tweeds with a thick, graying mustache, didn't seem as intimidated as the others. He strode over and took the chair across from Joshua without invitation. "You're staying in the village long?" the man demanded.

"Don't know."

"Are you staying here?"

"The other inn." Joshua motioned to the harried pot boy, who handed him his glass of ale. For a moment, he considered buying this nosy man a pint as well, but no, let Munro bond with this representative of the law. The man hadn't identified himself, but any criminal could spot one of his enemies in a few seconds.

Not his enemy here, Joshua reminded himself. He had nothing to hide and everything to find out. He'd have to act unnatural, but he let himself do it anyway. He held out a hand. "I'm from London. Smith is my name. You're not in uniform, but you're a constable, yes?"

The constable shook his hand but didn't bother to answer the question. "You know a fellow named Nathan?"

"Several. London's a big city."

"Very funny, Mr. Smith. And how odd you'd pick the same name as Mrs. Trout's late friend?"

"I didn't pick it. Was born with it."

"Any relation to her or, rather, her husband?" the constable asked.

Joshua pretended not to hear. "Why are you asking about Nathan?"

"Mr. Nathan also came here from London. He has met with an accident."

Joshua said, "No, sir, I don't know any such man. Is he still here?"

The man—Joshua recalled the gatekeeper had said their constable was Weaver—jerked up a thumb. "Last I saw him, he said he'd taken a room here. If I thought he were dangerous, I'd haul him to the police station."

"What sort of accident did he have?"

"He said he fell off a horse, but none of us seen him riding on one. He didn't rent a hack from any farmers. So I don't rightly know. He's a strange man. And as I said, from London, just like you."

"Who knows? Perhaps I do know him. Can you describe him?"

"Red hair, short. Swollen lip now."

"You think someone hit him?"

"I do indeed." The constable's gaze had never moved from Joshua's face, and his eyes were full of suspicion.

Joshua raised his hands and held them out flat, first showing his knuckles and then his palms. "See? I didn't hit the man. Beating a man leaves marks on the hands."

"No way to tell if he was struck by fists. Funny that you should know what happens to a man's hands in a fight."

"I admit to some fisticuffs in my past." Joshua wanted to appear friendly, so he avoided grinning. He'd been told that he looked menacing when he did—then again, that observation always came from people who knew the usual reasons his father might smile. Joshua did resemble Big Mervin. "Why's Nathan got your interest?"

"You know why. Mrs. Trout is a lady we admire and respect hereabouts."

"Glad to hear it." Joshua didn't lie. He liked the Ah Girl. "Word travels fast in this village if she told you about my visit."

"Never mind how I know what's what. Just take care you don't go stirring up trouble with us, or with Nathan, come to that."

"All right," Joshua agreed. He picked up his spoon, hoping the cop got the sign that he was done talking.

Just then, Munro came in the room. His gaze met Joshua's, and he smiled.

Joshua's hand hurt, and he realized he was clutching the spoon too hard.

That smile seemed real and warm with no trace of poisonous intent. The way it lit Munro's face made every other person in the room less vivid. They practically faded to furniture. Even the annoying cop was less alive than Munro.

Joshua wondered at the strange power of an exchanged look, and with a sense of dismay, he figured he'd caught what music hall girls and crooners were always rhyming moon and June about.

Disgusting that he should let himself fall into some sort of experience of the heart with a man. Worse, he'd made himself into a fool.

He was all alone in this strange little village, with no resources aside from Munro, who'd taken his leather coin pouch back in London, come to think of it, lifted it from Joshua as if he were a rube and failed to return it.

Their whole venture had been unpredictable from start to finish, which disturbed Joshua. He'd never much liked adventures or the unknown when he was a boy—life had been dangerous enough. This new situation created something unfamiliar, the fear in the pit of his belly almost exciting, a form of anticipation. He didn't trust it.

"'Scuse me," he muttered to Munro, who'd just approached. He got up and walked out of the room.

The constable watched him leave.

Joshua headed out the back of the inn, and the cool air made him shiver in his still-damp clothing. The privy was a far more pleasant setup than he was used to. Spring flowers bloomed in patches outside, and plants climbed up the sides of the wooden building. He did his best to ignore his state of half arousal as he pissed. His pecker was too eager lately. Best to shift his mind elsewhere, he mused as he buttoned himself up.

He'd find this Nathan fellow, find out what happened to Matilda, find a new path for himself.

As he walked to the inn's back door, a man stepped out of the shadows. Joshua didn't see him full-on, but had the impression of someone well-dressed and wearing a bowler low over an angular face.

In the dark yard, the lamp over the back door reflected off something in the man's hand. A knife. Perhaps he was going to go cut up a slab of bacon and simply held a knife as he walked toward the taproom, but then he moved fast toward Joshua. Instead of waiting for the attack, Joshua ducked and slammed his shoulder into the man's stomach, grabbing for the hand that held the knife.

With a startled woof of pain, the man slammed down onto the gravel path not far from the privy and rolled away.

When Joshua took a step closer, the man scrambled to his feet, cursed, grabbing the hat and knife he'd dropped. He seemed to have dark hair mixed with gray, but that and his bony face were the only impressions Joshua had of him.

"Well?" Joshua beckoned an invitation for another attack, but the stranger ran away without looking back.

Joshua considered chasing after the stranger who'd nearly attacked him, but he didn't know where the streets in this village went. It was a trick in London to anger a wealthy stranger and then let him chase you into a rookery where your pals would take care of him or at least remove his wallet. Those attacks usually included some insults. The utter silence of the man, who'd only let out a short curse and grunt, seemed ominous.

Joshua climbed the steep and narrow back stairs to prowl around the guest rooms. It took concentration to be stealthy nowadays, but he reckoned he did better than even a few days ago. All the exercise made his leg better, not worse.

There were five guest room doors, and he tried each one. Four showed empty bedchambers. The fifth was also unlocked, but there were signs someone had been there. He walked into the room when he saw drops of blood on the wood floor and smeared on a cloth next to the washbasin.

He looked under the bed and saw more blood and a pair of bloody socks. An impressive amount, but hardly the puddles that would come from a serious injury. Likely the Neely man must be reasonably fit if he could get away from the inn bleeding this much.

"What are you doing?" Munro's accent was more obviously Scottish than usual.

Joshua managed to hide his surprise and climb to his feet without much trouble. "Looking around for Nathan."

"I did that already. T'man's fled. An' that constable ye left behind is pestering me."

"Is that why you sound foreign again?"

"Perhaps." Munro came to stand next to him, then dropped into an easy crouch.

Munro's head was the same level as his crotch...Joshua swallowed. He grew even more aware of the other man's body as Munro leaned down to look under the bed, and his jacket fell forward, showing the wool trousers pulled tight over that bottom begging to be patted or swatted or just rubbed.

Munro said, "I didn't tell him that Nathan's left this room."

"Tell him?" Joshua wiped his mouth with the back of his hand. What were they talking about again.

"I didn't tell the pesky constable that the benighted Nathan is gone." He rose to his feet and brushed off his knees. "We'll go back down now? The stew will be cawld and I need to get back to the other inn, reet awa'."

He was unaffected by Joshua. The close proximity of their bodies had meant nothing. Then again, he didn't look at Joshua as they left the room and went down the stairs. And he stared down into the stew as they ate.

Joshua ate a few bites and put down his spoon. "I was attacked just now. Outside the outhouse."

"Oh?" Munro frowned. "You're not having me on? No? You seem far too calm about such a thing. Did you get hurt?"

Could a man be too calm? Seemed like a strange thing to fuss about. He held up his hand, looking for a sign of nerves. It remained steady. "No, but the man was almost as tall as I am, and he didn't have red hair."

"Anything else?"

"Well dressed. He carried a knife, but I don't know if he could use it well."

"How can you not know?" Munro's frown deepened. "Are you saying he didn't really attack you?"

"I didn't let him."

"Did you hurt him?"

"Not much."

That seemed to reassure Munro, whose face relaxed some. "What did he say? Did he have an accent?"

"He didn't talk more than a curse, which sounded normal to me."

"Londoner?"

"Maybe."

"Hardly much information to go on, eh? And look at you, just eating stew like nothing took place."

"You don't believe me?"

"I didn't say that. Should we tell Weaver about it? He's coming over to join us again."

"No." Joshua had no desire to be linked to violence in the constable's eye, even if it was violence he hadn't initiated. Had he, though? He'd operated as he did in London, expecting the worst of people. Perhaps the well-dressed man hadn't meant him any harm?

Well, of course he meant Joshua harm. If he'd been an innocent wandering about the inn clutching a knife, he should have grown indignant and demanded to know why Joshua had knocked him down. Instead, he'd run.

The constable had abandoned his spot he'd taken by the fire and came ambling back over. "I thought you two had fled the premises. I'd have to come after you for Fred Peters."

"Who's he?"

"Your host. The owner of this fine establishment." The constable pulled a chair over and sat without asking permission. "I never did get around to asking why you gentlemen are in the area?"

Joshua looked at Munro, brows raised, but of course, Munro seemed to be avoiding his gaze, hunting through his pockets.

He'd pulled a silver card case from his inside pocket and, after flipping through a few, extracted a card and handed it over to Weaver.

"What the hell is a lieutenant from Scotland doing on my turf?" He frowned down at the card. "That's the rank of chief inspector here in England."

"Chief inspector?" Joshua whispered. "First you're Sir Ross, and now you're a chief inspector? How'd you end up a sergeant in London, then?"

Munro carefully closed the case and put it back in his pocket. "I took an approved leave of absence to do research, a sabbatical."

"Research?" Joshua demanded. "What's a sabbatical? Something to do with witches?"

Munro didn't even look in Joshua's direction. He only paid attention to Weaver, who demanded, "Why the devil didn't you come to me right away if you're a cop?"

"Who's ta say I didn't pay a call on ye, Constable?" Amazing how Munro's eyes could go so cold when his mouth was quirked into something resembling a smile.

Joshua felt a burst of fondness—his Mr. Munro did relish skirting the truth. And intriguing how he sounded like a different man when he laid on the Scottish for Weaver. Joshua knew about switching back and forth between accents. Before he got his growth, any time he slipped and spoke like a toff in the rookerie, he'd be pummeled. Big Mervin boxed his ears when he slid into street talk.

But Joshua's shift in accent didn't seem nearly as dramatic as Munro's, whose whole voice changed, going lighter and higher when he spoke with the accent. Imitating his grandmother, perhaps.

"You'd best tell all you hae on Mr. Nathan," Munro said.

Joshua, whose survival had depended on reading the slight motions of bodies, could see that Weaver let Munro win. A quick glance away, a nod, and a shrug. He was the swaggering cock of the walk in this village, so he likely would be aggrieved, maybe come after Munro with claws out, ready to strike or give a pack of lies.

But Joshua had judged that one wrong.

"I'd share anything I know, but I can't figure him out," Weaver said. "It's deucedly annoying to have mysterious goings-on in the village and no way of knowing if they're dangerous or not."

"Don't I know it." Munro met him halfway, two lawmen commiserating together.

Interesting how quickly they both backed from a fight.

Munro added, "Naturally, if I discover anything, I'll let you know." He glared at Joshua. "Smith? Don't you have anything to tell the constable?"

"Not a thing." Joshua glared back. Luckily, Munro didn't push him to tell the story of the man with the knife. Joshua didn't want Weaver to poke around in his business.

Did the constable notice how Munro slipped back to a less exotic accent?

Weaver rose to his feet and held out a hand. "Thank 'ee. Since I know where you're staying, I might come to call." Now it was his turn to play with silly accents.

"Of course." Munro rose as well.

Joshua stayed in his chair and kept eating.

Once Weaver had gotten out of earshot, Munro sat again. "I think it best if we don't part ways after all. Come back to the inn with me."

"Why?"

"It might be that someone harmed Nathan because he was attempting to dig up information—which is what we're doing as well."

"And?"

Munro heaved a sharp, impatient sigh. "All right. Think on this. If Nathan's really one of Neely's men, a hardened villain from London, then he's not an easy person to attack. Who's to say the attacker won't come after one of us?"

Joshua said, "We're alert all the time. Just like I was in the yard earlier. Harder to get us."

"Nathan could be an attacker as well, in league with that one who went after you. How large a knife did he have? I saw an empty knife sheath up in that room."

"I didn't," Joshua admitted. "Are you sure?"

"It was a metal sheath for a hunting knife, about nine inches long."

Joshua wondered why he hadn't noticed. The blood on the floor and then the presence of Munro had distracted him. "That's longer than the blade the silent man held."

"Two men with knives out and about," Munro said. "Jesus, Smith, just come back with me."

He found he couldn't say no to Munro. They finished eating, and Joshua swallowed the last of his glass of ale while Munro went to talk to the bearded men. Judging from the shrugs and head shakes, he didn't learn anything.

When he returned to Smith's side, he gave another of his narrow-eyed frowns. "It's not too late to tell Weaver about the man who attacked you."

"I shan't." Joshua walked out the front door.

Munro followed, drawing his jacket tighter as a gust of wind pushed against them. "We need to discover his identity. Since he didn't come in to complain to Weaver about you, he had to have been up to no good."

"He was too nervy to be a real threat."

"You're absurd. We'll go back to the Archer and—"

"I'm not talking to Weaver. But I agree we should stick together."

Munro sped up to an angry trot, and Joshua, with his longer legs, kept up despite his limp.

They arrived at the other inn quickly, which was good because a few drops of rain fell as another storm threatened. The dark closed in on them, and though the bar here was a good deal tidier than the one at the last inn, the room was less welcoming, with a smaller fire and fewer patrons. Only three men sat together in the far corner, playing some sort of board game.

"Another glass of ale and the pain in my side will be eased," Munro said as he fetched the glasses and brought them to the table. "And I'll probably pass out snoring."

"Your side. Now I remember what the Winter boys did." Joshua shook his head. "It feels more like a week than a day, eh?"

"Two weeks."

The rain and wind picked up. Some drops flew down the chimney and hissed on the fire. Joshua yawned.

Munro pulled out his watch. "We probably won't get anyone coming to visit from Mrs. Trout's household, which is a pity. Maybe we should give up waiting."

He licked his lips, pushed the watch back into his waistcoat, and stared into the fire, very obviously not looking in Joshua's direction.

Joshua's exhaustion fell away. They'd walk out of this room and upstairs, just the two of them—up to a room with a bed in it. Something would happen when they were alone together.

Munro wanted him. Joshua could sense that as surely as he felt his own desire flow with every heartbeat. He sent up a prayer, *please let that be true and not just wishful thinking*, though who he thought he was praying to was a mystery. It didn't seem likely that the god Nicky and the Bible described would grant wishes to a man wishing to seduce another man.

He gave a snort of laughter, and at last, Munro glanced his way.

"What is amusing you?"

Joshua gave a half shrug. "Not sure I should tell you. Don't want you to run screaming from this place."

"Ach." Munro muttered something else Scottish, and leaned forward to look at the fire as if it were his worst enemy and he could kill it with his stare.

Joshua had felt this coil wound tight before, deep in his body, when he was in a room with a man he'd desired. This tension had seized them both for a change, and that made it ten times as distracting and a thousand times more interesting.

More time passed, but Joshua barely noticed. His mind was filled with pictures of Munro's body, clothed and naked. He imagined the sounds Munro would make, the texture of his skin, his hair, the scent and taste of his body—

"I'm closed now," the barman said. "Early night before market day."

They rose and pushed the wooden chairs back under the table.

Munro gave the barman thanks and some coins to pay for their drinks, and they went into the chilly hall, which was lit with only a single gas light on the ground floor.

The stairs creaked under their footsteps. Since he had the key, Munro went first, which allowed Joshua the pleasure of watching him.

As he unlocked the door, Joshua stood close behind him, not so close that their bodies touched, but he could hear the rasp of uneven breath and feel the heat of the other man's body. Munro stopped fumbling with the key and turned his head to say something. That was when Joshua closed the space, moving just a few inches forward.

His mouth grazed Munro's cheek, the stubble rough under Joshua's lips. Then he traced the few inches from that warm cheek to rest for a moment on Munro's mouth, so light a touch, he barely felt the soft flesh under his.

When Munro opened his lips, perhaps to say something, Joshua moved in, a tilt of the head to the side to fit better, and yet another inch forward. The perfect taste of warm man, and the hint of beer filled him. Munro's mouth opened under his.

This was a real kiss, eager and growing more so. The best and second kiss in Joshua's life. His mind, practiced at adding the value of figures and items, automatically put this in a black ledger of riches. He'd record it as a huge sum, the grandest he knew.

Munro made a small strangled sound, and Joshua withdrew at once, leaning away.

"Not in the hall, you ninny," Munro whispered, his words puffing warmth over Joshua's face.

Joshua wanted to clap and cheer, to scream alleluia, and most of all, he wanted a repeat of that kiss. Instead, he reached around Munro and pushed open the door. "Go," he growled.

Munro grumbled again and walked into the room.

Chapter Twelve

Munro walked to the fireplace. He squatted and lit the kindling logs stacked in place by the chambermaid. Out here in the middle of nowhere, they used wood, and the fire lit fast and burned hard. It smelled better than usual. Joshua thought everything smelled better, which reminded him that he wanted another long draught of Munro.

Joshua closed the door, locked it, and moved to the middle of the room. He wanted to go straight to Munro, grab him up and have him, but not without making the whole thing as clear as possible in this room thick with lust.

"You want me," Joshua informed him.

Munro stood up. "If we get this…this thing out of our systems, we might do better. Be better able to conduct the business we came here for, I mean."

"Yes. All right." Joshua licked his lips.

"So." Munro cleared his throat. He pulled at his necktie, loosening it, but not taking it off. "What do you want?"

"You."

"Do we touch?"

"What?"

"I mean, do we touch each other or only ourselves? And…" He cleared his throat again. "And watch?"

"Is that something you've done?"

Munro nodded again. "Not often. Not more than a couple of times. In school."

"I'd like that, I think. But another time. Now, I want you."

Joshua had gotten used to the dark. Did Munro blush? Or perhaps that was just the golden light of the fire.

"I—I…" Munro began. He fidgeted with his tie but didn't move otherwise.

Damn, he was going to back out of this. Joshua was about to say he'd do anything Munro wanted. Touch himself, watch, bray like a donkey, but God, something, anything, when Munro finished, "I don't think I'll last very long."

"As long as it takes," Joshua said. He wanted to close the distance again, but that would be Munro's job. So he took off his coat and draped it on the chair, too impatient to fiddle with the wardrobe. They'd only exchanged that kiss, and he needed more as soon as humanly possible.

He knew he had good arms and shoulders, so he'd use them to advantage. Nicky had once said something about birds displaying feathers to attract mates. Joshua smiled remembering that. He imagined himself flapping his arms like they were wings, and wanted to laugh.

"God, your smile," Munro whispered. "It's so pretty."

That did make him laugh, the croak he still hadn't gotten used to. "Pretty. Me?"

"You," said Munro, and he finally pulled off the bloody tie, and his collar too, exposing his throat. That dip erased Joshua's laugh and made him grow hard as a plank. A goddamn divot in a man's throat between his collar bones would do him in.

No, he was done in when Munro came to him and pulled him into an embrace, so tight there was not a bit of air between them, and their skin touched in so many places...but not enough. Never enough.

So Joshua loosened that hold on him and scrabbled at Munro's clothes, drawing a sharp "Ow" when he hit a bruise on his side. He slowed, but only a little, as he unwrapped his treasure.

Munro had known he liked men and had ignored it all his life—successfully for the most part. At school, he'd fumbled and played with another boy, but so many of the others did. It was experimenting.

He'd been with a woman once and had enjoyed the soft skin and heat of her body. But it couldn't have prepared him for the shocking sensation of Joshua Smith, crook and sodomite, running his hands over Munro's skin.

All day. Every minute of traveling with Smith, walking with him, and watching him. It all led to this. They shed their clothes in a fever of aching need that shriveled that insignificant word "enjoy" to dust.

Moments later, they lay together, face-to-face, and cockhead pressed hard to cockhead. Munro didn't want to spend, but he would soon if the slide and heat of Smith's body against his didn't stop. Smith reached between them and wrapped his hand around both hard cocks. Munro tucked his chin to watch that tight grip rise and fall, working them.

"Wait," he gasped and pushed up again, too close.

"Mm," Smith agreed and pushed him onto his back on the wide bed. Munro could breathe again until Smith used his mouth on his nipples to lick and tease. He lightly touched the bruises, and even the echo of pain seemed sensual because the broad fingers touching Munro belonged to Smith.

When those fingers gripped Munro's penis again, he arched up for more. He pushed his own forearm into his mouth to stop the groans of pleasure. Nothing could feel more astounding—until that hot, wet mouth came down on him and greedily sucked.

Please no, he wanted to yell. It's too good… But his own skin filled his mouth.

And then, just before he lost that last control, Smith moved up and off. "Not yet," he said. He pulled himself up and yanked Munro's arm away from his mouth and replaced it with his own hungry mouth and tongue. "I've been thinking about this too much for it to end soon."

Me too, me too, Munro wanted to say, but he couldn't speak.

He'd been too passive letting Smith take the reins, because it all led to his own pleasure. But now he explored as well, feeling the swell of Smith's flexing buttocks, the firm flesh of his back. When he touched Munro's slippery penis, he knew he wanted more than just touch. He wasn't too full below, he thought and smiled. The man would fill him indeed.

He spread his legs and invited a man into his body.

"Is it that simple?" Smith leaned back on his feet, gazing down at Munro with heat and longing so intense, the expression on his face might have been yet another caress.

"Saliva," Munro said. "I've heard it takes a lot of that."

Smith's wide grin was wicked. "You've heard?"

"I haven't done this either."

"Oh." Smith grew solemn. For a moment, his flagpole seemed to droop, but then he slid his hands along Munro's legs, up the insides of his thighs. He bent his head and began to apply the saliva directly where it belonged.

"That's...that's. Oh God." It was disgusting and glorious, down to every detail, the hot breath and touch on his tender parts to the brush of soft hair on his thighs.

By the time Smith had done a thorough job and moved up Munro's body to place the head of his cock to that hole, Munro had added that attention to the list of things he'd never imagined doing, never thought could be so glorious, and never wanted to forget.

The burn and pressure of Smith against his arse was almost too much, but then he got past the worst and then it was too much again, too much pleasure.

He wrapped his arms around the bulky Smith. His legs were already pressed up high. It was an awkward and wonderful position, and to realize there was another person inside him, moving...seemed unbelievable yet was utterly real.

"I'm engulfed by you," he whispered in Smith's ear. Smith pushed deeper, and that was the last coherent sentence either of them managed for a long time.

Smith shoved harder and faster, and Munro pushed back as the man inside him hit something—and that experience was added to his list.

Munro's orgasm hit hard and sudden. He couldn't move, but he didn't need to. Smith pushed and pushed it out of him. A few pushes later, Smith groaned and grew even larger inside him. One last deep thrust, and they cried out and groaned together. Any other time, Munro would have laughed at the strange chorus, but now it fit exactly, just as Smith did.

After their hearts slowed, they both got off the bed to clean up. Smith's limp was bad. "You have ruined me," he said with an exaggerated scowl.

"I'd apologize, but I believe you've done the same to me." Munro pretended to be in great pain as he clutched his side. The bruises hadn't hurt all this time, but the pain did seem to be returning.

They stood, naked in the middle of the room, gazing at each other by the light of the dwindling fire.

"I'm glad it was you," Smith said. The wet flannel in his hand, he looked Munro up and down. "I'm glad it was you and not some molly at that house."

"Ach. Well…" Munro began, but didn't know how to finish. Smith walked over to him and pulled him into an embrace.

"Ach wheel," Smith whispered in his ear. "You're welcome to more. Want to get back into the bed?"

Munro should have felt shoddy after their passion, but found himself saying, "Indeed. Yes. Please."Munro rolled onto his back and stared up at the ceiling. *Mistake. Mistake. Mistake.* The word click-clacked like a train car in his mind. He should have waited until…never. There wouldn't be the right time to indulge in this pleasure. He would never be the person who could let another man touch him and not eventually feel remorse.

He allowed himself a few minutes of regrets, lying next to Smith, listening to his long slow breaths that occasionally verged on snores. And slowly, the gnawing guilt seemed to slide into something less important. The urge to tumble out of the bed and run away eased.

Munro watched the weak orange light of dawn slide over the whitewashed walls and wished he could talk to someone about his confusion, though the only person he could speak to was Smith, and he didn't think that would be a good idea

After rising, he turned to look down at Smith, who lay on his stomach. The cover had pushed down far enough to reveal the interesting dips in his spine and the swell of his buttocks. But Munro's gaze shifted and stayed on the white and pink stripes that crossed Smith's muscular back. He hadn't noticed those marks the night before. Old scars, deliberate cuts…from a whip? A cane?

Munro thought of his own childhood. He had grown away from his family after he'd been sent to school, but he took his family's prickly love for granted. They didn't show their pride in him, but he knew well enough they possessed it.

But the man who bore those scars had a very different past.

On a good day, Smith's father thought of him as a commodity. The bad days…Munro suspected he saw the marks of those on his back. Amazing that a man raised like that had a core of decency and even a warmth—or the appearance of those qualities.

Munro wasn't sure he trusted Smith enough with his own weaknesses, but a tenderness filled him when he recalled the man's gentle and not so gentle kisses, and the way he laughed. Smith showed more than animal hunger last night. The way they'd fallen asleep, wrapped in a clumsy but comfortable embrace—that was more than lust, perhaps even more than the need to banish loneliness.

Munro reached out to trace the line of a scar, then drew back his hand. Before his weakness for Smith overcame his resolve, he turned and walked to the box room to get dressed. The drab little room with his leather satchel on the bed reminded him of their travel north, which helped bring him back to his purpose.

If Munro's telegram to Kelly about the death of Matilda Neely satisfied her father, then they could return to London. The thought made him gloomy. He reminded himself that he hadn't failed this woman. Her death was due to childbirth—that seemed consistent in the stories he'd heard.

But of course, as always, the other guilt rose: Becky MacAllister, beaten and strangled in Perth. The sergeant had urged Munro to keep that monster in jail for a while more, and he hadn't listened. His sense of failure had become a familiar sensation, rather like sorrow, marching side by side with it. Becky's sad end would be a part of him always, and there was no point in trying to shed it.

It would be interesting to discover the red-haired stranger's reasons for coming to the village—and for hanging around. This Nathan character had shown up in the village just before they had. And then there was the other man, the one who might have attacked

Smith. Munro longed to know his identity, and to discover what Nathan knew that Munro didn't. Munro had to find a way to locate the man, and then get him to confess his reasons for pursuing Mrs. Smith.

As Munro buttoned up his waistcoat, a tremendous pounding came at the door to Smith's room.

Munro rushed to open it before Smith woke, but it was too late. Smith sat up and began to climb to his feet, slightly clumsy. He limped to the middle of the room, naked and bleary with sleep. His hair stood on end, and Munro wanted to go smooth it down.

"That wasn't you banging?" he asked Munro.

"No."

The knocking started up again.

"Urgent bugger. Best see who it is." Smith yawned, grabbed his clothes from the chair, and strolled to the box room. Munro took a moment to gawp at his naked form. What a champion form it was too. Smith might be shaped a rather like a block, but it was the sort of block that inspired Munro to consider ignoring the frantic knocker, ignore the reason he'd come north, ignore everything to chase after Smith and see how well the two of them would fit on that smaller bed.

Not the eager mind of an investigator in search of truth.

He made sure the box room door was shut before answering the bedroom door.

A slight red-haired man with extravagant muttonchops barged into the room before he noticed Munro.

"Beg pardon, sir. Wrong room." Panting and trembling, he turned to leave.

Before the man could take a step, Munro reached over and grabbed him. The arm under Munro's hand was lumpy—from a bandage wrapped around it. The man yelped and pulled back from him.

"I didn't mean to cause you pain, but I need you to answer a few questions, and—hey!" Munro let go and stepped away when the man flourished a knife at him.

The box room door slammed open, and Smith raced toward the man, who turned his attention and knife in Smith's direction.

Munro grabbed up the pitcher from the wash stand and brought it down on the man's head.

With a groan, the stranger reached up and sliced his own ear before he dropped the knife and collapsed to the floor.

He whimpered and curled into a ball. "What kind of cosh did you hit me with, you bastard?"

Munro checked the pitcher, which had a smear of blood but no other damage.

Smith leaned over and picked up the knife. "Fellow has a head made of stone. And seems you were right about his knife," he told Munro as he held up the blade, which was clean. "But I'd say that's about ten inches."

The man rolled back and forth a few more times. Still clutching his head, which was bleeding, he finally stilled and blinked up at Smith. "You're Mervin's boy. Thank God." He reached out a blood-covered hand as if he would shake hands, or maybe it was a request for help getting to his feet.

Smith raised the knife in a menacing pose. "Who're you?"

"Nathan." Still on the ground, the red-haired man smiled and gestured at the knife. "I won't use it on you. Can I have it back?"

"Of course not," Munro snapped. He grabbed a towel that lay near the washbasin and handed it over. "But you can sit up and wrap your wounds."

"I'm bleeding?" Nathan sounded shocked. He took the towel with trembling fingers and pressed it to his head. "Blood!"

"That's rich from a Neely man who carries a hunting knife that could kill a wild boar."

"I wouldn't use it on you. I just said that, din' I?" Nathan started to get up.

"Sit." Munro pointed at the floor. "Stay still. And tell us why you came knocking at the door this early in the morning."

"It's near seven."

"Talk."

Nathan checked the towel, then put it back against the head wound, which trickled rather than spurted blood. "I was looking for Mr. Smith there. I wanted to talk to him about something private."

Smith's face went blank, the look that Munro had thought meant stupidity but now believed meant anger—and danger, because he mustn't forget that Joshua Smith had survived a world that destroyed weaklings.

"Go on," Joshua rasped.

"Private," Nathan said.

Munro shrugged and walked to the other room. He'd listen, of course. He could even watch through a crack.

A moment after Munro nearly closed the door, Nathan spoke. "I want to join your gang. I'm handy with the tooling and the dubs—specialize in lifting tickers. I got skills and I got some information. How do I join the Smiths?"

"Why did you pull a knife?"

"A fellow can't be too careful."

"Did you follow me here for this?"

"No, I came to this bloody town looking for Matilda Neely, erm, Smith."

"You here on her father's orders?"

"Not so much. But see, I was her guard back in London. I knew all her friends and knew all about this Mrs. Trout."

"I asked if you were sent here by Neely."

"No. I wouldn't tell him about Trout. I didn't want to rock his boat. He's bloody angry about Matilda, for some reason, even after she got married. To you, I mean. I want to stay out of his way. In fact, I'd like to stay out of his way forever. I heard tell of you and thought why not. And why I'm looking for you, see, is he got some flea in his ear that I was the one who fathered that baby of hers."

"Were you?"

"I was drunk. We all were, all three of us. And she'd had wine too."

Munro had to control himself from barging back into the room and shaking the bastard Nathan as a story came out about a girl and three men in her father's organization. No wonder the poor girl had been so afraid.

"Did Neely know about your party? That why you're running away?" Smith sounded only curious, not horrified.

"I, uh. I don't think she'd tell him. We knew where she lived after she married you, and we made it clear it would be a bad idea to bring up our names. Or any names. Really."

"So you raped and then threatened her?" Smith was still curious, but now there was an edge to it.

"Well, it wasn't like that. I mean we all had a good time. It was friendly like. And it wasn't a good idea to talk about it."

Joshua made a growling sound that might have been a word, but Munro couldn't make it out.

Nathan hastily continued. "All in the past, in the past. And you helped her out. Thank you for that. I would have married the girl, but if I'd said as much to her father, then he'd know what happened with her. I was in a bind."

"Nothing like the one you left Matilda in."

"No, no, of course not." There was fear in the man's voice.

Munro peered around the door and saw why. Joshua's heavy brow was thunderous, and he held the knife expertly—and pointed at Nathan, who sat with one hand up and the other holding the towel to his head.

"If I could do it again, I'd leave the girl alone. Let her try her experimenting with other men, I'd say."

"What do you want?"

"You're close to your father, next in line for being the boss."

Was that possible? Munro wished he could see Smith's face better to interpret the response he gave these words.

"If I was?" Was that an admission by Smith? Why hadn't he said something about his privileged position with Big Mervin? Although, come to that, why would he? It should have been obvious—he was Mervin's son. And more to the point, Munro and he were not close friends, not truly.

Nathan went on, "You might put in a good word for me. Tell Big Mervin I'd be an asset."

"What if I ain't going back to London?"

"That's plain nonsensical. 'A course you are."

"Might I remind you who has the knife? Why are you here in town? Why were you looking for my wife?"

Nathan said something that might have been *dunno*.

"Did you plan to threaten her again? Or drag her back to her father?"

The man flinched. Munro didn't see a lot of details in his narrow view of the room, but he saw that flinch.

"Awright. I've heard tell she had something important."

Smith waved the knife in a small circle, but Nathan remained silent. "Tell me," Smith growled. "What did she have?"

"I came looking, but she's dead now, and it's gone for sure. And if Neely thinks I know about it, he will blame me for the whole thing. He's mad as a hornet and looking to blame anyone. He sent out detectives and blokes in his gang, all sorts to find the girl and…the whatever. If we come back with the information that the girl's dead, I don't know what he'll do. Though I don't think he'd worry about her death none. It's the other thing. That she took."

Munro wondered if a bloke from the Neely gang was the one to try to go after Smith.

"You have ten seconds to tell me what that thing is she took. Ten. Nine. Eight—"

"Dunno! Dunno! It's that secret none of us know, but she took it from his safe in his office. Soon after she married you, I heard. Oh and I heard it might be gold. Or maybe jewels. Or maybe books, you know, information. The minute Neely figured it out, he sent a party to search your place."

"I thought our apartment had been searched."

"Only thought? You weren't sure? Ha. We did a good job at that."

"What did you find?"

"Nothing, including not Matilda. Her da went insane with rage. He hired more people, yes, I mean us, and outside detectives too. So many people out looking. Keeping watch on you too, in case you took off, but you stayed put."

"Go on. What else does Neely know or suspect?"

"Since you Smiths were watching us, and you told your Smith people she was gone, now there's even more looking for her. Here in this place too, since someone came after me. Makes a fellow nervous. I know it weren't you who attacked me, but I thought some of your people would figure out the way she traveled north and come looking. But here's what I want. I want to form a team with you. We'll find Neely's treasure and take it back to your father. If he has something important of Neely's, that will help him win the war."

"I don't know about a war."

"With Neely and you Smiths. It got calmer because you married Matilda, but it won't stay that way. Neely wants a chunk of Mervin's pie. I want to go in with you. Neely is a crazy bastard."

"Could be he shows you his crazy because you raped his daughter?"

"He doesn't know about that. And it wasn't rape. The girl enjoyed it."

"Might he think you ruined his young daughter?"

"Ah. Well. But he didn't much care about her anyway. I mean he was fond of her in a way but didn't really know her. He didn't know about that showgirl who was her friend, the lady who's Mrs. Trout. Didn't know the first thing. Not like I did. Not like we did. We cared for her."

"That's why you got her drunk and fucked her."

"That's not the point. It's all in the past."

"I'd hoped she had someone who cared. I truly did. It's sad that you're it." The disgust in Smith's voice was raw.

"I cared for the girl."

"She died, maybe having your baby, and you're only interested in making deals with my father."

"What are you, some sort of Weeping Wanda? She died a week after her baby."

Hadn't it only been days? The number did seem to change.

"I'm not dead. This is how I stay above ground. Don't seem like a pious type, Smith. That's not the sort of man you are. I know about you. You be vicious, mean enough to kill your own brother."

Smith didn't deny the accusation. He didn't ask what Nathan meant. Munro's blood went cold. Could all that sorrow he'd demonstrated about his brother Nicholas be guilt?

Smith certainly sounded vicious as he answered, "I won't help you for free. You understand that sort of thinking, hmm?"

"I don't have money, not so much as a return ticket to London, so what do you want?"

"Information, starting with who attacked you. A description would be good."

"I don't know. He came up behind me in the dark. And I was too happy with liquor to see well enough. Here now, can I sit down?"

"You are sitting."

"On a chair."

"No. Stay on the floor. Who attacked you and why?"

"I told you, I don't know. First I thought it was one of the others who work for Neely, but I dunno. Whoever it was came up behind me. I let my guard down 'cause we're not in London. He walloped me, searched me, took my wallet, left me on the street, if that lane going out to nowhere can be called a street. I hate this village."

"Did you tell the constable? I know he's met you."

"O' course not. Think I'm an idiot? He's a copper." The man sounded positively insulted.

"We're not in London, as you keep saying. He might help."

"Not going to any copper. Not here, not anywhere." He leaned forward. "Speaking of such things, you are thick with that Scottish cop. What's going on there? Hmm? You and he?" He gave a coarse laugh. "I don't care. What a man does for pleasure is his business. But a cop? You and a policeman?"

"No. We came here to find my wife."

"You think I can't tell?" He drew in a long breath. "Smells like men in here, if you catch my meaning."

"I think it's time for you to move along. I'll keep this good knife."

"I was just having you on. I won't say a word."

"Do you think I care what you say about me?"

"Oho, you have a care for the Scottish cop, then?"

Munro waited for Smith's strong response—would it be a denial or the start of a drubbing? Instead, Smith only gave one of his croaking laughs. "A god-fearing type like that? Wouldn't touch the likes of you or me with a ten-foot pole."

"Not what I'd say."

"Ah, well, you say otherwise in London or anywhere else, and he'll have you drawn and quartered. You know he's by way of being some sort of lord. All sorts of power. Don't poke that bear unless you want your head ripped off."

It was a long speech for Smith. A strange one too.

It seemed to take the wind out of Nathan's sails. "Just kidding around," he muttered.

"Well, time to move on. You go on back to London. Here. I'll give you a note of introduction even." Smith got a piece of paper and began to hunt around, probably for something to write with.

Munro appeared then, carefully closing the door to the box room behind him and, after watching him search for a time, handed him the stub of the pencil.

Smith scribbled on some paper. He wrote quickly, with none of the hesitation over each word Munro saw in the poorly educated.

Smith handed the note to Nathan. "Take this note to Mr. McLeevy, the lawyer. See what it says?"

"Can't read," Nathan said cheerfully.

"Says to offer you work. You might tell him I'm fine, working on family business."

"Yes, yes, thank you."

"Here now." His voice dropped to the menacing growl again. "Any mention of Lord, um, Sinclair, and I'll do for you, understand, Nathan?"

"For certain. Yes."

He should have stayed with the uninterested and amused tone, but perhaps Smith knew that Nathan would do better with a mix of friendliness and threats.

Munro walked Nathan all the way down the stairs. The man glanced nervously over his shoulder at Munro. "Have a safe return to London," Munro told him.

Nathan squinted at him and winced.

Munro said, "If I were you, I'd check with the village doctor to see if you're fit to travel."

"Do you think I might get my knife back before I go, sir? Your lordship?"

"I doubt it," Munro said.

Someone was walking down the hall. Munro gave him a small push to get him to leave before anyone else spotted Nathan. "Get yourself to a doctor."

He returned to find Smith combing his fingers through his hair in an attempt to look tidier.

"Do you think it's a good idea that we let him go?" Munro went to his bag and fetched his brushes.

He handed the brushes to Smith, who examined them closely before gingerly pushing one of them through his thick dark hair, watching himself in the mirror.

"You want me to tie him up? Gut him? I don't trust him enough to keep company with him. I figure if he sticks around here, we can find and follow him. This place is small enough it shouldn't be too difficult. He found us. We can find him. If not, you can bribe the station master to see if Nathan's heading back to London."

Munro hummed a little. "It's something of a plan. Though I'm hoping to return to London once I get word from my employer."

"Oh?"

"Aren't you interested in going back?"

Smith shrugged.

"When you talked about me. And you…" Munro paused, trying to hunt for the right words. Smith didn't help, so Munro continued. "You sounded angrier than I'd have expected."

"He's an underling."

"Do you mean that sort of tone is what he'd expect?"

Another shrug.

"I just wondered if you were trying to hide what we did." He paused again.

This time, Smith had something to say. "Of course I'd hide it."

"But did you do so for my sake or yours?" Munro realized that sounded sadly insecure and hastily added, "That's hardly important. It's good that you quash rumors. It could be dangerous for either one of us."

"Hmm," Smith agreed, calm as usual. "The Winters would pay to hear you and I are together here."

"Yes. Though that speech you gave him about my power— oh, and why on earth would you call me a lord? You know I'm not, yes? Perhaps it will create greater trouble than I had before. If he thought I had a great deal to lose, shouldn't I worry about a man like that or his friends coming to me and demanding blackmail money?"

Smith only looked at him and grinned. "No. He's more frightened of you than Neely or Smith."

Munro gave up. "And frightened of you, as well."

"I bloody hope so." Smith held up the impressive pig-sticker of a knife. "Like my new toy?"

"Not at all." Munro's wicked angel must have whispered to him. "I quite prefer your natural length of hard iron to that."

Smith's mouth dropped open, and several heartbeats later, he began to laugh. He seemed to have trouble breathing, he laughed so hard, and Munro thought he heard him gasping, "You! You said that! What a surprise you are." He wiped his face with his sleeve, which needed a cleaning. "But don't be saying any such thing too loud. And never around others, eh?"

Munro folded his arms. "Of course not. I'm not an idiot."

They walked downstairs to find breakfast. The innkeeper brought them tea and then hurried off to order food from his wife. He seemed nervous. Had he overheard them the night before? Had Weaver warned him about them?

"What'll we do, then?" Smith asked.

"We might try to find out what your wife took from her father."

"That satchel," Smith said to himself.

Munro waited, but Smith said nothing else. "Aren't you curious about what was in it?"

Smith shrugged. "I have ideas about where it might be."

"Well?"

He shook his head. "Naw. I'm likely a lunatic. I'll let you know."

"I'll stay here and wait to see if I get any more instructions from my employer and perhaps some of Mrs. Trout's servants or friends come find me."

Smith's shoulders seemed to relax as if Munro had taken a weight off him. "Then I'll go out. For a walk."

Munro was about to ask where he'd go, but the innkeeper appeared with a toast rack. His wife brought out plates of tomatoes, fried eggs, and black pudding.

Smith picked up the teacup properly and didn't bolt his food.

"No need to stare like I'm one of the show freaks." Smith wiped his mouth with the napkin. "I was made presentable, remember?"

"Maybe I was staring for another reason." Munro hadn't been, but this talking bravely was so new and interesting to him, he couldn't help himself.

Smith carefully replaced the teacup in the saucer and picked up his fork. "No," he said. His voice was thin as a whisper. "You stop. You can't have changed so much in just a few days, days no, hell did you change overnight? Did you abandon all your good sense?"

"I am paying you back for your forward behavior in your apartment. I understand now how freeing it is to act like an uncouth rudesby."

The ghost of a smile touched Smith's face, but he went back to eating his breakfast.

In a normal voice, Munro asked, "Where will you go on your walk?"

"Maybe see if Nathan got on the early train back to London."

"I should go to the station as well and see if the telegram came there rather than was delivered here—" He wiped his face and looked around for his hat.

Smith almost jumped to his feet. "I'll go now. See you soon. Good luck." He put on his hat and walked away before Munro had put down his own fork.

It hardly took advanced detective work to understand the man didn't want company on his walk. Perhaps he had some private instructions for Nathan.

Munro drank his tea and wondered about Smith's secrets.

He waited an hour and then another, then grew restless. Hanging about waiting for information to come to him was absurd. He walked out into the quiet lane that passed for a main thoroughfare in this town. Several women with baskets hurried past him. Market day, of course.

He'd go there and see if anyone might provide more stories about Mrs. Trout or Mrs. Smith.

As he strolled around the corner toward the square where the Jubilee fountain and market day carts had been set up, he heard a babble of excited conversation. He stopped to listen when he heard the words "dead body."

And then a man talking to his friend about the death pointed excitedly. Good enough for Munro—who was still a policeman at his core, no matter how other parts of him had shifted since meeting Smith. He walked quickly in the direction the man had pointed.

Chapter Thirteen

The buzz of activity came from an alley leading from the market. Not everyone in the crowd had noticed the hullabaloo, but a few craned their necks to see what was going on. More people walked in that direction and he sped up, knowing that a crowd could destroy evidence. Munro paused only to regain his balance when he slid on the cabbage leaves and horse shit on the cobblestones.

He had to blink as he entered the alley, flanked by buildings looming so close that it never saw the sun. It might not reek the way that rookerie had, but the sight of the body lying next to a tall brick building brought back the fear he'd felt so recently.

For a horrifying moment, he thought it might be Smith and ran toward the sprawled figure. Several men stared down at it, all standing, none squatting down to offer aid. The reason they didn't bother became clear as soon as he drew close and understood the puddle around the body wasn't from the rain the night before.

The man's throat had been cut. He lay in so much blood—he must have met his end here. Some bloody footsteps led away from the body. Just as he noticed that they were very large footprints, the body went from being a grotesque portrait of a gaping throat to an identifiable person.

Munro stared at the wisps of red hair sticking up from the scalp, and the far brighter scarlet streaks on the pale skin. Nathan, the Neely man from London, wouldn't be boarding any trains on his own. As Munro stared at him, another man's name churned through his mind.

Smith. The son of a violent man, the product of a violent world. Smith, the man who had suddenly slunk off on his own and who had seemed extraordinarily worried that Nathan would squawk about the sodomite.

Munro cleared his throat, swallowing down the bile flavored with the black pudding he'd just eaten.

What lay before him was police business, and he was, at heart, still a policeman. Never mind that he had no authority—he had to do something familiar or risk making a display of himself being sick.

He carefully moved closer to the body and felt the man's head and looked at the puddles of blood.

One of the men stepped near, too close to the blood.

"Stop right there, sir," Munro barked. He straightened and ordered another man to fetch Weaver while he stood guard over the corpse and prayed that he was entirely wrong about Smith's activities in the last few hours.

Munro didn't like the coincidence. This man had visited them, made nuisance appeals and threats to Smith…and now he lay dead not so very far away from their inn.

Munro's hands and mouth tingled, and he knew he breathed too quickly. He forced himself to calm. He must think.

When Weaver showed up, Munro gave a report. He laid out the few facts he had, adding that the murder had to have taken place after the rainstorm.

That nettled Weaver. "I know that, sir." He paused his scribbling in the occurrence book and looked up at Munro. "Can anyone vouch for where you've been for the last couple of hours?"

"The innkeeper."

"What about your friend? Smith?"

It was Munro's turn to pause. "I'm not certain where he is at the moment, but you should get his story from him." It was the best he could do—not tell a lie, and not point a finger directly at his "friend" Smith.

"I'd best do a more thorough examination." Weaver scowled at the body as if he were annoyed at its ruining his morning. "And then take more statements."

Munro leaned against the brick wall and watched Weaver work. For a man in a rural area and likely not much experience, Weaver did the job well. He nominated a friend of his to guard the body, then quickly interviewed the men who'd made the discovery. He took lots of notes and asked pertinent questions. Munro wasn't sure if his efficiency made the situation better or worse.

Weaver carefully pulled a piece of paper from the man's pocket, the note Smith had given him gone scarlet with blood.

"This is ruined. We won't get a thing from it," Weaver said with disgust. He laid it on the ground. Munro almost suggested that they wait until it dried to see if the marks would show, but he found he didn't want to draw any attention to Smith.

Munro followed Weaver as he walked around to the market. No one he spoke to had noticed the man in the market square and, since he was a stranger and had red hair, certainly one of the regular stall holders would.

They walked back to a spot in the sunshine, near the alley where the body lay.

"Do you have anything to add, Sir Ross?"

He said something of no use about how it was a pity there were no witnesses, then added, "What will you do next?"

Weaver wiped his bloody fingers on a cloth and tucked it into his coat pocket. "I'll go to the inn where he was staying, though last night, Fred said he complained about the place not having proper locks on the doors."

"Oh?"

"Yes. And when I stopped by there this morning to check on him, Nathan didn't answer his door."

No one would accuse bloody Weaver of shirking his duty.

"You were worried about his injuries?"

"Yes. But it puzzles me where Nathan could have gone. On market day, there aren't many places that will serve a man breakfast. I wonder if he came to the Goat and Grapes?" As Weaver spoke, he watched Munro closely. "He wasn't present when I came down to breakfast. You might speak to Mr. and Mrs. Summers. They'd have noticed him earlier."

"When do you think he died?" Munro asked. Was his manner too casual? Too stiff? He had to force himself not to wet his lips, though his mouth had gone dry.

"Do you have a theory?" Weaver watched him, perhaps testing him so he'd have to tell the truth.

"Not recently. I felt the body. He's cool to the touch, and the blood is not fresh liquid." Munro spoke carefully. He didn't lie, but he wasn't telling the whole truth. He had put Smith's safety above a murder investigation, and he wasn't even sure if the man he protected was innocent.

He made a silent promise that he'd personally drag Smith to the lockup if he proved guilty—and throw himself into the cell next to him.

His hands felt awkward, his feet glued to the ground. Every piece of his body seemed to scream out the fact he'd withheld facts about Smith. But the guilt he supposed showed on every part of his face must not have appeared obvious to Weaver, who only nodded. "I'll look around here some more, then come over to the Goat and Grapes soon enough."

"Will you?" Munro managed.

"Perhaps we can put our heads together and find some answers," Weaver said. "I'll have to send word to the chief and the coroner." He narrowed his small dark eyes at Munro. "I suspect this crime has a connection to London." He might as well have said Gomorrah his scorn for the city was so obvious.

Munro tried to relax his breathing but found he couldn't. "You believe the perpetrator came from London? As well as the victim?"

He must have sounded offended, not frightened, because Constable Weaver raised a placating hand. "Perhaps I'm wrong. Although carrying out a murder on market day suggests someone who knows our ways. Easier to hide in such a big crowd."

A hundred people hardly constituted a crowd for a man used to London.

Weaver walked back to the body for another look. Munro considered staying to meet the coroner but decided he'd best find Smith and begin the most desperately important examination of a suspect he'd ever conducted.

***

Joshua was naked from the waist up, washing up in the washbasin in the room, when Munro came crashing through the bedroom door.

"You're here," he said, then stopped dead to stare at the grimy water. "That's blood."

Joshua nodded. "Nicked my hands a few times."

"With…with a knife?" Munro sounded horrified and looked pale enough to keel over.

"Here, what's wrong with you?" Joshua picked up the shirt he'd been wearing that had gotten covered with dirt and found a relatively dry patch to rub over his body and hands. He gave Munro a bit of a leer. "Need to lie down for a time? I can help you relax."

"Where did you go? You need to tell me exactly where you've been and what you did there. Be specific." He picked up the shirt, walked into the box room, and then reappeared a moment later, a heavy frown still darkening his good looks.

The calm Munro had vanished entirely.

"I didn't peg you as the jealous type," Joshua joked.

"You need to tell me. Sharpish, Mr. Smith. No messing about. You left the inn—after making sure I didn't follow—and you had a definite goal in mind. Tell me what you did."

Joshua picked up a clean shirt, the only one he had, and put it on without bothering to pull up his braces. He walked to the chair in the room, a rush-bottomed rocker, and sat. The sense of triumph that had filled him vanished, replaced by a sense of dread and, to be fair, a touch of disappointment. He'd expected to tell his news and be congratulated.

He asked, "What do you think I did?"

"You need to talk to me, Smith. I'm not playing games here."

"Neither am I. You think I did something horrible. What is it?"

"Nathan is dead."

"Neely's man? That's a pity." It was, a bit. He really should have checked with a doctor the way Munro insisted. Though, to be honest, his death helped solve a problem of potential blackmail that he'd worried about—and then the truth hit him. "He was murdered, and you think I did it."

"He was murdered," Munro confirmed. He began to pace. "I saw the body. He had his throat cut. And I could tell by the angle of the wound, a very deep wound, by the way, that it was cut by someone taller than he with a great deal of strength. Someone likely stood behind him and didn't get sprayed with much blood. A tall man with strength who knows how to commit murder with a knife—that's who killed him."

Joshua's gut twisted. He should have known that he wouldn't escape his past when it came to this man. And it made perfect sense that he wouldn't be able to. After all, Munro barely knew him.

Munro was still talking. "Weaver thinks the killer came from London."

"Weaver? You talked to that nuisance?"

"He is the local law official, carrying out the investigation of a murder. Of course I talked to him."

"And did he see that stuff about tall men who know how to cut a man's throat? Or did you tell him? Did you say anything about how Nathan hinted at blackmail about sodomy? And pushed me into writing a note? Oh and the note. They'll find that. You say how I left this place this morning without you?"

Munro didn't answer.

Joshua rose to his feet and began to pick up his belongings that lay strewn around the room. He'd be damned if he'd stick around and be nabbed for a murder. He'd had vague dreams about leaving London, even vaguer ones about being a companion to this man who was so different from him, yet someone he felt closer to than anyone since Nick. Bang went those dreams, about as dead as Neely's fool with a throat cut in some village.

The idea of walking away now hurt more than it should have, which made him angry. He'd been a fool to think he could be close to anyone, especially a policeman with a preacher's soul, no matter how dirty and funny that man could be in private.

Joshua was Big Mervin's boy, and now he'd learn to do what he should have long ago: put up those good thick walls.

When he went to fetch his dirty shirt, he realized Munro had locked the door to the box room. The bloody cop was collecting and preserving evidence. Joshua tried to feel angry but only managed sorrow.

"How soon you reckon Weaver will be here?" he asked as he fastened the buckle on the bag that held his few belongings.

"Did you kill Nathan?" That voice was deadly calm now, with a quaver of preacher's fury.

"If I said no, would you believe me?" He saw a few pennies and a sixpence on the wobbly wooden table near the bed and went over to sweep them up. It wouldn't get him as far as London, but he'd get some money from Munro, even if he had to hold him upside down and shake him to get it. "It was probably the drunk man who attacked me last night."

"The one no one else saw," Munro said. "The attack you were far too calm about."

He pocketed the coins and turned to Munro. "Well? Would you believe me?" he challenged.

"I—I don't know. God above, I hope you're not the one. I don't know."

Joshua heard pure anguish. That wasn't the cold and determined cop before him. It wasn't fury in Munro, but pain. And maybe his pain was for Joshua—unless he'd made friends with that Nathan fellow this morning and mourned his loss. That thought almost made him smile.

He dropped the bag and considered going to Munro, but he resumed getting dressed, tucking in his shirt, pulling up his braces, finding his waistcoat, sliding his arms into it and carefully buttoning it though there was mud on it as well.

"Are you going to tell me what the hell you were doing that got you filthy and made you bleed?" Munro was all fire and determination again.

"I was visiting a grave."

Munro stopped walking and folded his arms. "Go on."

"It just didn't seem like anyone had a real story, you know? About my wife."

"What do you mean?"

"I'd hoped she wasn't there. Wishful thinking, I expect."

"Why the hell are you covered with mud and blood?" He was listening. Still upset but listening. "Did you go there and..." His mouth dropped open.

"I visited the grave with a shovel."

"Did anyone see you?"

"Didn't get in by the gate, didn't see nobody there."

"You went and dug her up?" Munro's voice cracked on the question.

Joshua grabbed his coat and pulled it on. "Nearly right."

Then he went to the wardrobe and opened it. It was empty except for a battered metal box covered with mud and a few smears of blood. He pointed to the box, in case Munro didn't get the point.

"She might be in the dirt down lower. I dug and got a foot or so down before I hit this."

"What is in it?"

"Dunno. Didn't look. I expect it's what she stole from her father."

"The object Nathan mentioned." Munro stared down at the box, gray eyes wide. "That has to be why he came here—he was looking for Neely's box—and why he wouldn't leave. And why he said he wanted to join up with your gang. He was looking for it and thought you had it."

This was better. He was catching on, and the sharp angry look was directed at the box, not Joshua. "What made you think to go haring off to Mrs. Trout's place?" Munro asked.

"Struck me as odd how nervous the lady was."

"Yes, yes." Munro knelt to examine the box on the shelf. "You're right. I noticed that as well. And the footmen who came crashing into the room—that's not normal."

"Then she didn't want us hanging about."

"But the grave. Why on earth did you think to return there?"

"She sent that footman Stephen to watch us."

Munro hefted the box, which was heavier than it appeared it should be, and put it on the floor. "And how was that decision enough to get you to take the risk of digging a hole and desecrating the grave?" His tone was excited, not judgmental.

"She had to hide it in a place she could find it again. And I wondered, why did she need to be so worried about that spot that she sent a footman along to watch over us?"

"I thought the escort was just to get us off the premises."

"Oh. That, yes."

"Do you mind if I look at the box?" Munro wiped some mud from his hands on his handkerchief, then used the cloth to wipe at the lock.

"You already are," Joshua pointed out. "But keep going."

"I need my satchel." Munro held out a hand without looking away from the box He seemed to have forgotten his anger and suspicion. Joshua wasn't about to remind him of it.

Joshua handed over the bag.

Munro rummaged around and pulled out a scrap of leather that he carefully opened to show some picks, as nice a set as any cracksman would own. He inserted a betty and jiggled as if he picked locks every day of his life.

"Pretty work," Joshua said. "Not one of my greatest skills."

"I beg of you, forget you saw me do it and don't remind me of this moment." Yes, that was more like what Joshua wanted to hear: some teasing, a hint that there'd be a future for them, and that grin Munro flashed him.

The lock popped open, and he pulled it off.

Joshua said, "Nathan told me he was good with the picks too. We'll never know if he lived up to that bragging."

Munro opened the box.

The scent of earth and mold filled the room. Joshua, careful of his leg, sat next to him on the floor. Something round and yellow glittered in the boggy mess inside the box. "Is that gold? Yes, it's a sovereign."

Munro peered close. "I think so, and there are some reddish and green things that must be jewels. And if those ledgers are intact, they might be even more interesting."

The brownish sludge Joshua had thought was mud and leaves in the water turned out to be books.

Munro stood, holding the still-muddy object. The box full of gold, jewels, books, and water was heavy, and he carefully lifted it, then tilted it to pour the brackish water into the pitcher.

He tried to remove one of the books and cursed when the waterlogged item ripped.

"I'm afraid to let it dry like this in case it sticks together in one great pile."

They finally wedged out each book with their hands, lock picks, and the late Nathan's long knife. By the time the box was empty, six books of different sizes, though all bloated with water, lay on the rug. Some were cheaply made. One was leather.

"Damn and blast," Munro muttered, as he carefully peeled open a page to show there was nothing but ink smears. "It's illegible now, but it's obviously a ledger. And the other one I ruined was a book of addresses, I believe."

Joshua whistled. "No wonder Neely's in a panic. If these are his records, he'd hold them precious. Gold and jewelry can be nicked. Information's harder to recover and more dangerous to lose."

He eyed the pile. Yes, the box's contents would have fit in Matilda's satchel before the paper grew thick and heavy with water.

Munro squatted by the books, carefully examining each page. Joshua watched him work. His own thick fingers didn't have that deft ability to separate pages. After about a half hour, Munro gave a happy cry. "Some of the ink near the binding in the middle of these two are intact. I don't like tampering with evidence, but this…" He sliced the pages out and laid them carefully on the bed, which would now smell like dirt. Then he stepped back and smiled down at the pages. "Now they won't dry stuck together."

Someone knocked at the door. Munro looked at Joshua, who shook his head and mouthed the words *don't answer.*

He rolled his eyes and backed into a far corner after Munro called, "What is it?"

Mr. Summers cracked open the door. "Constable waiting to see you downstairs, Mr. Munro. And if you've seen Mr. Smith, would you ask him to join you?"

"Thank you. I'll be down directly."

After Summers shut the door and the sound of his retreating footsteps died away, Joshua spoke. "No. I'm not meeting that man."

Munro turned to him. "You're innocent of killing Nathan, and that's the crime he's investigating."

"I got no witnesses. No one saw me this morning at Mrs. Trout's place—I made sure of that." Joshua didn't try to hide his impatience.

"I understand, but you didn't do the deed, and we should help the constable discover who did. After all, you and I agreed that the murderer could come after us next."

Joshua wouldn't even try to explain to this clear-eyed gulpy. Who knew a cop could be such an innocent? "You go on down. I'll stay here and guard this stuff. Nathan's death might be tied to it, eh? So best to keep an eye on it. Maybe the killer will come looking." That thought cheered him a little. "I'd like to have another go at that coward from last night."

"I think it best if I tell Weaver about what you found, though."

"What? What the hell?" Joshua sputtered.

"How can this upset you? I don't see any possible objection. Weaver is not the killer, and he's interested in seeking answers. When we have sincere and well-trained people looking, the more likely we are to find out what happened."

And there it was, the widest gap between Munro and him, such a glum realization. That innocent fool thought that the cops had the agenda of justice and not finding easy targets.

"You go on down. I won't," Joshua said. "He thinks I hold a candle to the devil."

Joshua knew something about his nature—his hair? his posture? his name?—riled most police. Perhaps they felt his suspicion of them, a distrust set deep in his bones that rose to the surface and showed in his eyes. His mother had died in prison, but it likely started before he was born. As far as he knew, his father's father's father was a thief.

Sergeant Munro had struck him entirely another way from the start—likely because he was the only cop not smashing fists and clubs into Joshua that night. It could have been the fact he'd called off the dogs with truncheons. Maybe his voice with that accent meant a new world, or it could all be purely physical—the way he made Joshua hot with lust. *Chief inspector,* of all things.

Munro pushed back his jacket and put his hands on his hips. The posture that was supposed to display disgust only showed his natural grace, not to mention those large hands bracketing narrow hips. A bolt of desire near nobbled Joshua, hitting him like a clout. And he hadn't known such a thing could be as crippling as any blow from a fist.

"Go on," he urged again, a bit huskier than usual. "You can tell him."

Without a word, Munro gathered all the gold into a clean handkerchief—except the piece Joshua had secretly pocketed. He twisted the handkerchief closed and grabbed one of the less soggy books and left the room.

If he hadn't seen that look of suspicion on Munro's face, Joshua would have demanded a kiss, but that canny man might have tasted his intentions. He'd have known it was a goodbye kiss too.

The metal box, Nathan's murder, the contents of what might or might not have been a grave—it was all family business, Neely and Smith business. Joshua had married a Neely. No constable could do what Joshua planned.

He crept into the corridor but froze when voices came up the back stairs. Unless he wanted to be seen, there was only one way to go out.

The window didn't open very wide, but he managed to unlatch the metal fastener and shoved it wider.

The stable yard below seemed a long way down and the building's brick sides smoother than when he'd examined it earlier.

But the wall had missing mortar here and there. He'd had plenty of practice climbing.

In less than five minutes, he was on the ground and hurrying away from the inn.

***

Weaver waited for Munro by the fireplace, which was dark and empty on this warmer day. He rose from the comfortable chair and shook hands with Munro, then frowned at the entrance. "Where's your friend? I heard he'd returned to the inn, covered in mud."

"You have the most amazing sources of information. I nearly forgot what it was like to live in a village. No hiding any sort of secrets."

"Isn't that the truth. Where is he?"

"Cleaning up."

"Interesting." He frowned at the newel post at the bottom of the stairs, as if willing Smith to come down and join them.

"This is even more interesting." Munro held up the soggy book. It was a cheap ledger, and the pasteboard binding was falling apart. He put it on the table next to Weaver's chair. The handkerchief of money and jewels clinked as he dropped it by the book.

Weaver stopped looking for Smith's entrance and paid attention at last. "What is all this?"

He knew well enough how guilty it made Smith look, but he would have to start somewhere. "I believe it is what Nathan was actually in search of when he came to this village."

Weaver opened the scrap of cloth and, after touching them, leaned back quickly, as if the coins and gems might bite him. "Were you in search of it as well?"

"No."

"You were asking questions about Mrs. Trout's friend. From all reports, that's just what Nathan did. Is there a connection to this? And is this what you were in search of? This money?"

"No. We only wished to find out what had happened to Mrs. Smith. That is all. Do you think that if we were searching for the gold and jewels to keep them, I'd show you?"

Weaver didn't seem to pay attention to his question. "And here is something else that I've learned. Nathan was at the Goat and Grape, seen coming down the stairs. I think he was visiting you."

"Yes." He tried again. "And by showing you this treasure, I admit as much—how else would I know what he'd come to the village to discover?"

"All right, we'll assume neither you nor he is lying about knowing each other in London. I'll give you that, Sir Ross."

"Thank you." Munro gave a mock bow without rising from his chair.

Weaver raised a finger. "But I have more questions."

Munro should have practiced what he would and wouldn't say to Weaver, and he thought of all the reports he'd delivered when he was a constable. That official tone wouldn't do if he wanted to pretend he felt casual interest and wasn't up to his neck in this affair.

"What sort of questions?"

"Why do you suppose Nathan was sneaking around rather than visiting you and Smith in a more normal way?"

Munro shrugged. "Perhaps he made his way in the world as a second-story man or some such thing. He was involved in less than savory business."

"And he confessed all this to you?"

"No. I overheard him speak of his background and recognized the names he gave of his acquaintances and friends."

"To whom was he speaking? Your friend, Mr. Smith?"

"Yes, and before you jump on the train of thought that Mr. Smith is the murderer based on that brief exchange this morning, 'twas a civil conversation. They parted amicably. Now to get back to your original point, apparently Nathan entered the inn without anyone noticing, and perhaps he even sneaked in, though by habit or intentionally, I cannae say. But into the inn he came. And I listened tae the conversation."

He took in a long breath and reminded himself to stick to an English public school accent, and to leave out the story of Nathan and his knife.

The fight over that knife… Could Smith have gone after Nathan for the attack with the weapon? What if Smith had found him in possession of the box, killed him, and then pretended to have found the box in the grave?

A wave of nausea rolled through him as he understood the truth might remain hidden because Munro had grown so befuddled by lust, he let the object of his desire get away with murder.

Except he couldn't believe that Smith could have been that crafty or underhanded. He hadn't known the man long, but he had seen nothing but honesty from him. A bent sort of honesty, but it seemed to go bone-deep.

Weaver was speaking again. Munro, lost in that onslaught of gloomy doubts and mawkish reassurances, had to interrupt him to ask, "Beg pardon?"

"What else did you hear during that conversation?"

He did a quick edit of the conversation. "They spoke of the sad young lady who died at Mrs. Trout's place. They discussed the fact that her father was eager to find her."

Tell him, the still-sane part of himself urged. *Tell him you were actually hired for that.*

No.

He was in for a penny, in for a bloody pound—but now he discovered he'd gone in for Smith, and not for justice nor the hunt for truth.

Weaver said, "You claim your friend didn't kill this man Nathan, who seems to have some connection to Mr. Smith, unlike anyone else in this village."

"Smith was attacked last night by a man taller than Nathan."

"Why didn't he report the crime?"

He didn't report crimes to the police, but Munro decided that wouldn't reflect well on Smith.

"The attack wasn't serious, not like murder," Munro said. "It might have been an angry drunkard. And back to the important

171

investigation, while Nathan was being murdered, Smith was busy digging up the box, and it was at least two miles off in the country, on the Trouts' property."

"How did he know where to dig? I should like to see that site for myself."

"I'm not certain how he got the information. I might ask him the same thing." That last sentence wasn't a lie.

Now Munro itched to get back to the room and bellow at the man responsible for transforming his staid self, a person who knew right from wrong, into someone less reliable. Becky MacAllister and Joshua Smith had changed him.

After he got back upstairs and yelled at Smith, he would get some reward for twisting the truth.

"He might be secretive, but I'm certain he didn't kill Nathan. He was too busy delving around in the dirt." He prodded the book and felt a wave of relief when he realized an obvious truth. If Nathan had had it first, he would have picked the lock and dumped the water. "This is too waterlogged to be freshly wet. It must have been under the ground for more than a few hours. Once we establish the spot where he discovered the box, then you'll be able to see that he walked too far and worked too hard digging it up to have the time to return to the village and murder Nathan."

Weaver folded his arms over his chest. "I still would like to speak to him."

As would I, Munro thought. He said, "I'll go fetch him." Then he'd have time to fill in the details of what he hadn't said to Weaver.

When he got to the room and found it empty, his first instinct was to pound down the stairs and out the door, perhaps borrow Weaver's shackles to lock up the blasted malefactor.

He walked to the bed and sat for a moment, trying to think where Smith could have gone. Then he realized that several of the books and papers were no longer on the bed. Smith had carried them off.

Smith had no money, so there was no way he could leave the village unless he walked away—not likely with that leg of his.

172

But the gold pieces… Munro hadn't counted them. What a fool he'd become in the presence of Joshua Smith—a blind, besotted idiot.

It seemed likely that Smith had fled to London with the papers to give his father all the advantages over Neely that the late Mr. Nathan had promised.

Munro considered telling Weaver everything and perhaps encouraging him to wire to another station and have Smith removed from the train and taken into custody. But that wouldn't get answers. For two long minutes, he sat and thought of what he should do—minutes he should be running and calling out for help to find a miscreant.

He went back downstairs. A plump, well-dressed man stood by the table where Weaver still sat. The stranger was introduced as Mr. Hawk, the surgeon. He shook hands with Munro. His limp fingers were remarkably pale and soft for a surgeon.

The two others explained the situation while Munro quietly fumed about bloody Smith.

Hawk said the coroner was several hours away, so he'd act as a middleman. They'd have to hold an inquest, silly though it seemed to Mr. Hawk. "It's not as if he could slit his own throat. But as you requested, I've arranged to have some photographs taken, Constable."

"Good, fine." Weaver rose from the table and turned to Munro. "I must go examine the scene of the murder with Mr. Hawk. I'd be grateful if you'd join us and tell Mr. Smith the same. Where is he?"

"Not here."

"I take it from your grim face he didn't leave word." Weaver grabbed his hat, a nearly shapeless felt thing. "He's not cooperating with my investigation."

Munro laughed without humor. "I make it my duty to go find him and tell him that and plenty more."

"If I had an extra officer, I'd send him after Smith. This doesn't paint a good picture of him."

"I am aware."

"As for you…well. Are you going to help me on this case?"

He thought of the way he'd left off so many facts in his explanations to Weaver. He still didn't want to explain those failures. Instead, he'd find answers. "I think the best way to help you is for me to discover where Mr. Smith has gone. I'll verify my suspicions about where he found the box. But if I'm wrong, and he didn't travel any distance to find it, or if the mud on the box somehow doesn't match the mud on his clothing, you can place him on the very top of your list of murder suspects. And I shall be more than happy to drag him to your lockup."

"His clothing might well be laundered or thrown away. And we hardly have experts who can match mud for mud."

"I know of someone in London who can do the work," Munro said grimly. "And I saved the shirt he was wearing when he returned after digging up the box. It might prove useful if a case gets to the Queen's Bench."

"You haven't been entirely certain of his innocence after all?"

Munro decided it was a statement and not a question—he didn't answer.

Weaver, who was about to go out the door, paused, his bushy eyebrows raised high as he examined Munro. "You are angry."

"Aye."

"Don't kill him. Or if you do, make sure it's in another borough."

Munro laughed, this time with actual amusement. It was kind of Weaver not to give him holy hell. He wouldn't have continued to trust a person who'd behaved as Munro had—prevaricating about a friend's activities until that friend had a chance to get away.

"Here now, Mr. Munro, if you'd like to save some time, take my horse. She's the dappled mare—still saddled and ready to go in the back of the inn's yard," Weaver said. "I'll tell Neddy it's fine."

"Thank you." Munro grabbed his hat and a coat, since the day had turned gusty and cloudy. He stalked out of the inn, ready to go on a hunt.

Chapter Fourteen

Joshua strode through the countryside more cheerful and lighthearted than he'd expected to be anytime that day or week. Before he'd set off, he'd paused a moment outside the inn's door to listen and stayed long enough to hear his friend Munro had lied for him, or rather hadn't revealed the whole truth about the "conversation" he'd had with the murdered Nathan.

When Joshua overheard that Weaver wanted to see the site where he had dug, he realized he ought to go warn the Ah Girl what was coming and maybe find out a few facts for himself. He left his satchel on the station platform, far away from the baggage carts, then jogged down the narrow streets that opened onto the impossibly wide, open fields that still made him feel a trifle dizzy, as if he stared down from a great height.

It felt good to run—his leg barely hurt him now. It delighted him to be finally growing healthy and strong again. All right, much of why he felt almost happy had to do with the spirited defense of himself he'd heard from Munro. Joshua wasn't fool enough to think they might dally together more than the night before, but it warmed him to think that Munro seemed to trust him.

Trust was a rare and expensive commodity in Joshua's life. He didn't see himself using it for any gain, but it was pleasant to know he'd acquired it. He'd hoard it like any miser, he thought as he jumped over a stile and picked his way through patches of grass across a field.

He knew the mud was deep at the far end of the field and trotted close to the trees to avoid the dirt. Funny how much better this world smelled after a rain shower. In London, the resulting stew of rain water and garbage reeked.

As he'd done that morning, he veered through the trees and avoided the path with the big iron gate and its guard. A stone wall surrounded the Trout property, but he knew how to climb those easily.

By the time he presented himself at the front door of the property, he was out of breath, waiting for the sound of hoofbeats, the pursuing Weaver's cry, but he heard nothing but the wind and a bird in the trees near the mansion.

Likely the Trout ladies weren't at home, which would be just as well. He considered turning back to warn the gatekeeper. Joshua had stolen items in his life—usually wallets and top hats. Digging up the box seemed more serious, perhaps because the tombstone had loomed over him as he dug, perhaps because two powerful men, Neely and his father, would have killed to get the contents.

He heard rustling in the bushes and stealthily drew his knife from its hiding spot inside his waistcoat. No need to pull out Nathan's showier too-large blade.

The knife was hardly going to help him, however. There stood Mrs. Trout with a revolver.

"How the blazes can I get on with life if you people keeps popping up here like organ grinder monkeys?" Her hand shook a little as she aimed it at his chest.

"I'm here to warn you," he said.

"Seems like I'm the one warning you."

"No, I'm not making a threat." He held his hands up in surrender. "I have a debt to pay."

"Go on, get inside, then," she snapped at him. He opened the door and peered around the hall. No footmen came to meet him.

Mrs. Trout followed, but from several lengths back. He couldn't turn and grab the gun from her. He considered turning and flinging his knife, but he'd wait to see what she had to say.

"Go on down to the sitting room," she called. She held the gun and reached back with the other hand to shut the heavy front door, never shifting her gaze from him.

He kept his hands in the air and walked backward so he could watch her. "Where's Stephen?"

"Who?"

"Your footman. Stephen and the others."

"Never you mind that. They'll come if I shout. You just go on into the sitting room."

177

He obeyed. With an exaggerated limp, he headed into the room she indicated. He strolled past the chairs and stood next to the carved marble mantel.

Her gaze shot to the wood and fire irons, and she shook her head. "Get away from there," she said.

He took three steps backward.

"And from there too." This time, she seemed focused on a large Oriental vase at his side. She must be nervous about putting him near anything that he might use to attack. If she was this worried, she ought to call for one of her guards, but she didn't.

"Where should I go?"

She glanced around the room, then gestured to a high-backed chair with her revolver.

He walked over. Before he sat, he reached behind him, under his jacket, moving very slowly. No reason to startle a woman holding a revolver.

"What are you doing?" she said. "I know how to fire this."

"I have something to show you." He carefully removed the oilcloth he'd tucked into the back of his trousers and laid the bundle on the carpet, then pushed it in her direction with his foot. The mud he'd tracked in got on the cloth—and now he saw he'd tracked it on the carpet too.

"What's in there?"

"Account books. They're from the box Matilda brought with her. Mr. Neely's secrets, I expect but don't know. They're ruined."

Her face went very red as she stared down at it. "Let me see. You open it," she ordered.

He slowly leaned over and flipped open the cloth.

She gave a small cry. "Where'd you get that, then? Was it that bloody Nathan?"

"I found it where you buried it. Tell me, is Matilda under the earth there too?" He folded his arms. "You did a bad job keeping it safe. Were you going to sell that box to the highest bidder? Good luck with that now." As he spoke, bitterness in his voice, he drew the knife from his sleeve again.

He hadn't thought he would attack, but the idea that poor Matilda, driven by fear, seeking shelter from a friend, had been murdered just for a load of coins and paper suitable for blackmail made him want to hurt someone.

After all, he had taken that damned oath when he married Matilda.

"What are you talking about?"

"You knew what was in the box. You recognized it. You know its value. It wasn't just a load of rubbish and some coins to you, was it?"

"Of course I know what they were." She still stared down at the books. "Ruin't, ain't they." She sighed and slowly lowered herself onto the sofa, facing him. "Still, as long as you kept your mouth shut, Neely and the others need never know they're no use to anyone." She raised her gaze, and those large expressive eyes flashed anger. She moved the gun back and forth a little. "I can keep your gob shut for you, you know."

"Are you going to try to blackmail Neely?"

"Well, of course," she said, sounding offended, as if he were an idiot.

"You might get more money from Smith."

"Your father, you mean? Are you acting as his agent? That why you're here? I shan't sell to him."

"Why not?"

"Don't be daft. He wouldn't help me."

"Help?"

There was a thumping in the hall. She rose quickly to her feet and turned to face the door. Joshua saw his moment. He leapt to the sofa, hitting his leg against a small table and knocking it over. He grimaced in pain but managed to grab the wrist of her gun hand. Holding the knife near her throat, he growled, "Drop it." The revolver fell with a thud on the carpet—and didn't go off.

That was all well and good. He began to relax and tried to come up with a reasonable explanation for Weaver as the door opened.

He'd expected to see the constable, but instead it was the older, plump Miss Trout, an amiable, nearly blank expression on her face as she came in the room.

"Did I hear noises?" Her expression didn't change when she caught sight of Joshua. "Oh dear. It's another one?"

She ambled over to them, stopping a few feet away when she saw the knife at Mrs. Trout's neck.

Miss Trout tsked, and her vague smile vanished for a few seconds. "Oh, that is too, too much. Really more than enough."

Joshua opened his mouth to answer when he spotted another gun. This one in Miss Trout's hand. "You lot have more firearms than my family does," he said.

"Put down that knife, sir." Her peculiar smile had returned.

He lowered the blade but didn't put it down.

"I am quite serious." Miss Trout's hand was far steadier than Mrs. Trout's had been. "You will put down the knife. We have had quite enough of your sort tramping around the place, acting as if you were in charge."

"Please, no more," Mrs. Trout said, her upper-class accent and voice back in place. She held up her hand. "Not another word, I beg of you." She twisted and looked at Joshua. Her mouth trembled, and her eyes were wide with fear. "Do it."

He put the knife down next to the book on the floor.

Miss Trout made a tutting sound. "We really cannot have dear Matilda bothered by these people. This one will have to go before he hurts her." She had that amiable expression on her face again.

A cold shiver ran up Joshua's spine. This woman was a lunatic. Munro would have stood there and observed the scene with his hands behind his back, rocking on his feet a little, looking interested.

Joshua wanted to howl and grab up his knife. "I apologize for grubbing around in the grave, but I had to find where you'd buried the objects she'd brought with her from London."

"You had to," Mrs. Trout murmured. "You thief."

Miss Trout caught sight of the books. "Those came from her box? And she'd put it by the headstone? Such a clever girl. She told me they'd put it in an appropriate place."

"She?" He looked at Mrs. Trout, who was shaking her head at her sister-in-law—who ignored her.

"Matilda, of course," Miss Trout said. "She didn't want to have it on her person when she left."

Relief flooded him. "She's not dead. You didn't kill her. The grave, all of it was just to keep her father away from her."

"I suppose. It was their plan." Miss Trout tilted her head at Mrs. Trout. "Was that the plan?"

Mrs. Trout looked miserable as she nodded. "I thought it would end the trouble. Matilda was so afraid and angry, she wanted to bring down her father and every man around him. She wanted him to suffer. But I talked her into leaving well enough alone and simply…disappearing. We thought the gravestone would be enough to convince anyone. We even paid extra for a nice one."

"She's safe, then."

"As long as we keep awful men away from her. All the awful men." Miss Trout raised the hand holding the gun. "You thought we killed her?"

"I wasn't sure. The stories about her death shifted like lies."

"Dear Mrs. Trout wouldn't hurt a fly. I am a different creature altogether, though no, I wouldn't kill her. But you? One of those dreadful predatory creatures who makes poor girls like Matilda, like my dear Mrs. Trout, suffer? Yes. I'd take care of ending you."

Joshua cleared his throat. "Like you did Nathan?"

Her smile broadened. If there wasn't a strange gleam of insanity, and if she'd been about forty years younger, she might have looked coquettish. "Did someone kill him? I wonder who."

Mrs. Trout said, "Nathan? That odious man with the red hair? Dead? Where?"

Joshua said, "Just off the village square."

Miss Trout looked at her sister-in-law with that same coy smile. "I know you thought 'twas I, dear, but there. See? You know it wasn't my doing. I don't leave the property alone."

She cocked her head and studied Joshua. "But here we are at home, with this fool bothering us, poking his nose where it's not wanted. That's an entirely different story. Do you think your Mr. Reed would mind if I made a mess in the sitting room?"

Mrs. Trout gave a nervous giggle. "Aurelia. Please. Your joke is hardly in good taste."

"I am not joking."

Joshua was about to rush the older woman, but he heard a commotion outside.

Munro came striding into the sitting room.

Miss Trout turned in that direction, still holding her revolver.

"Sir Ross!" Mrs. Trout gave a shriek and ran to Munro. Joshua wished he could do the same.

Munro patted Mrs. Trout on the shoulder, then started when he saw what Miss Trout held. "Ma'am, lower your weapon, if you please."

Miss Trout scowled. For a very long moment, Joshua thought she had had enough and was going to blast holes in them both. But then with a long sigh, she pushed the gun into a pocket in her skirt.

And then, as if she hadn't contemplated shooting anyone, she walked to the chair by the fireplace and lifted her knitting. Munro stared at her. "What is going on?"

Mrs. Trout gave a tiny sob, a sound straight from the stage. "Your Mr. Joshua, or rather Mr. Smith, is threatening us."

"Is he?"

Joshua thought it best to hide the knife again.

"What are you about, Mr. Smith? What did you come here hoping to discover?"

"I came because I wanted to discover the truth of the ladies. I wondered if they killed my wife."

Miss Trout gave a high-pitched bark of laughter. "You are absurd. Your wife? You didn't spend two minutes alone with her. She told us. You couldn't possibly have a care for her."

Joshua smiled despite himself. "More than you'd think. More than I'd have guessed myself." Nicky would have been proud to hear him admit it.

Munro walked over to Miss Trout. "Your weapon, Miss Trout?"

"No."

Mrs. Trout said, "Please, Aurelia? We agreed that we didn't need any more trouble."

With a muttered comment about interfering men, she put down her knitting and rose from the chair, moving quickly for an older lady. She pulled the gun from her pocket and handed it to him.

Joshua eyed her but spoke to Munro. "They say that she's not dead. Matilda is alive."

"Where is she?" Munro demanded.

"We shan't say," Mrs. Trout said. "We agreed to protect her."

Munro folded his arms and leaned against the wall near the door. "If you won't tell us where Mrs. Smith fled, we will comb records and interview the stationmaster and others to discover her location. If you'd rather we didn't make your private business known to everyone in the village, you should just tell us."

"You do what you must. I shall keep my promise."

Joshua decided that he sincerely liked Mrs. Trout and grinned at her. She drew back, recoiling as if he'd promised violence. She told him, "If you should find her, then I beg of you not to tell anyone, Mr. Smith. Most especially not your father or hers."

Miss Trout chimed in with, "If you tell anyone, I will kill you." She paused with a bright smile. "Not I, of course, since I don't like to travel. But I will see it done."

"Is that how you contrived to have Nathan killed?" Joshua asked as if inquiring about the weather. She was so odd—perhaps if he didn't treat the matter seriously, she might answer as casually.

"Not at all." She paused in her knitting. "How did he die?"

"It's hardly the topic we'd want to discuss—" Mrs. Trout began.

"Throat cut," Joshua said.

Mrs. Trout paled. "Oh dear," she murmured.

Her reaction was strong and didn't seem to be part of her usual dramatic exaggeration. Could it be she recognized something about the cause of death?

Munro might have caught that as well. He studied her as he went into detail. "Someone came from behind and slit his throat, a fast, efficient way to kill a man. I'd suspect the killer had done it before and had very strong nerves, especially to do such a thing out in the open, not so far from a busy marketplace."

He turned that stony gaze on Joshua. "I don't imagine there are many people in this village who'd be able to remain so cool."

"I told you where I was this morning," Joshua said.

"Yes. You did. And before I came here, I stopped to examine the grave. There are signs it has been tampered with." He shot a brief smile at Joshua, but it wasn't the warm, intimate look Joshua had seen on his face before.

Mrs. Trout rubbed her forehead as if she wanted to erase the lines of perplexed fear from her face. Joshua again wondered what she knew that they didn't.

"Tea," Miss Trout announced. "It will do you good, my dear. Order some. Reed must be back from his errands by now."

"Yes. Yes, that would be good. Ah. Oh dear. I shall ask Stephen to bring us some."

She went to the door.

"The bellpull is broken?" Munro asked.

"Ah. Yes, indeed," she said. "Excuse me. For just a few minutes." She slipped from the room, leaving them alone with Miss Trout, who didn't look up from her knitting again. She hummed to herself, the half tune she'd been humming the day before.

Joshua crossed the room. He stood next to Munro and wished again he could lean against him, just as Mrs. Trout had. Or at least move closer and breathe in his scent and feel the warmth of him. Joshua was not a fainthearted man, but he had been spooked by Aurelia Trout, and the way she ignored them both and stabbed at the yarn with her needles didn't help him feel better about her. He muttered to Munro, "Miss Trout is calm under pressure. And she is tall for a woman."

"She is...unusual. As long as she stays put with her knitting, we can wait."

"Those needles are sharp."

Munro snorted. "I happen to know you have a knife or two that are sharper."

"Thank you for not telling Weaver about the fight Nathan and I had."

"How did you know I didn't?"

"I listened a little back at the inn."

"Despite the fact that I was going out of my way to not mention unpleasant facts to the constable, you still left. You knew he wanted to talk to you and yet you fled."

Somewhere in the house, a door slammed.

"Why did you think I fled?" Joshua asked.

"You packed your bag. You vanished. I wasn't sure. I-I didn't know what to think."

His clumsy way now was not based on thwarted desire or hurt feelings, and when Joshua understood, he was startled. "You talked to Weaver that way yet still thought I'd murdered Nathan and stolen Matilda's father's box from him?"

He shrugged. "Do you blame me? You know how to use a knife. I know you took some of the gold, which meant you could leave at any time you wished."

Joshua's disappointment transformed into anger. How could his Mr. Munro doubt him again? The one man who seemed to look for the good in him. The man who brought out the good. He wanted to say all this. He'd ignore the strange older woman in the corner and point out how much that distrust struck hard, particularly since he'd just been celebrating the way Munro had believed in him.

But then he drew in a long breath and let it go again. Of course it wouldn't be that easy. There were the seeds of trust, the

185

seeds of true affection. If he bellowed back, he'd just stomp the hope of growth into the mud.

And there was the truth of the matter—he had taken a coin from the box, but only to pay for a ticket on a train to escape.

"I didn't kill anyone. I didn't want to run away from you," he said as gently as he could, sounding almost as eerie calm as Miss Trout herself. "I didn't trust Weaver to find the real murderer. I wanted to be prepared to leave the village if there were signs he would come after me."

"You didn't trust me to find the truth?"

"You? Perhaps. But you're not the face of law in this place. I've seen what happens with the police. They say a man has no reason to worry if he's not guilty. About as much true meaning as a bunch of starlings squawking. In London, I'd be safe because of Mr. McLeevy's work and my father's connections. Here, I got nothing. I wanted to protect myself."

Silent, Munro pushed away from the wall and put his hands behind his back. Miss Trout's gun formed a bulge in his jacket pocket.

"Where has Mrs. Trout gone?" Munro suddenly asked.

Miss Trout looked up. "Getting tea, of course."

Hoofbeats drummed on the ground not far off, a horse going faster than Joshua was used to hearing on busy London streets. Munro went to the window but apparently saw nothing. He came back to stand near Miss Trout. "How long would it take to order tea?"

"Most of the servants take market days off, although I expect they're returning."

"The staff in the market," Munro said. "Bloody hell. Of course." He bolted for the door.

Joshua considered following him, but he still didn't think the strange Miss Trout should be left alone. How bleeding peculiar that Joshua of all people would assign himself the job as some sort of deputy of the law.

He walked to stand next to Miss Trout. "Did you order one of the servants to deal with Nathan?"

"I would have," she said calmly. "But I didn't. Where has your friend dashed off to?"

"Don't know." He listened hard. In the distance, he heard a carrying female voice, one that had been on the stage. So that meant Mrs. Trout was still on the premises and wasn't the one who'd fled.

Then he heard Munro's voice, just as loud and far angrier. He moved to the door, then paused to look back.

"Go on," Miss Trout said, without looking up from her knitting. "I expect he is on his way to pay a visit to your wife. I should have figured it out, you know."

"What are you talking about? Who's on his way?"

She only smiled at the yarn.

Chapter Fifteen

The house had been built in the last century, so Munro suspected the layout was designed to make it easy for the staff to serve food. He rushed for the door at the far end of the large dining room, hoping it led to the servants' hall, and was relieved to see he'd guessed right.

He entered a dark corridor and sped along without allowing his eyes to adjust. That was why he nearly knocked Mrs. Trout over as he ran.

"Ah! Sir Ross, what are you doing here?"

"I should like to know the same of you."

"I was on my way back to the sitting room. I'd, ah, visited the kitchen."

"Good, you can show me the way."

"I shall do no such thing. I don't want you disturbing my servants."

"There aren't many here, I understand. Market day?"

She attempted to steer him back the way he'd entered.

Trying to sound gentler and more patient than he felt, he said, "I'm sure it was alarming to have a knife held at your throat, but I assure you that I and my friend Mr. Smith are not trying to hurt you. We need to understand who killed Nathan. I don't think it was you or Miss Trout."

"Of course not. And my dear sister-in-law wasn't lying about leaving the grounds without me as, ah, an escort." She gave up trying to push him along, and they walked side by side in the corridor, though there was barely room. "That alone proves that she didn't kill Nathan."

She slowed her steps and seemed to be listening.

"What are you waiting for? Will the tea tray be coming in this direction?"

"Tea? Ah, tea. Yes. I'll go make sure… You'll wait with the others? Yes, that will be best."

Her manner and all the "ahs" settled the matter. He ignored her and took off at a run.

When he got to the kitchen, it was empty.

Mrs. Trout hurried up to him. "Stop making a fuss, if you please. If you must yell, let us go into the butler's pantry where there is some privacy."

"There's no one here."

"Cook is in the garden. I will speak to you in Reed's pantry." She led the way to a well-organized small room off the kitchen and closed the door behind them.

"All right, tell me what you know," he demanded.

"I beg your pardon?"

"One of the footmen might have done it, I expect. They're more like guard dogs than anything else. You or your sister-in-law would have decided that Nathan was a threat and sent one of them after him. Stephen would be tall and strong, and he said he'd worked for a butcher. He'd know how to efficiently dispatch animals."

She reared back and raised her chin. "You have no right to come uninvited into my home. You said you were no longer associated with the police. You have no right at all to act like one."

"Miss Trout and you carry guns. You must feel under a threat, and it must be related to Mrs. Smith since you have only recently hired those rather unusual footmen. You were afraid of Nathan and the way he nosed around."

"Says the man guilty of sticking his nose in other people's business."

"I'm trying to be of service to Mrs. Smith, nothing more."

"She turned to me for help, not the likes of you."

He allowed himself a smile. "She found a good ally with you."

She seemed to relax a little until he asked, "Did your help include murder? Did you hire someone to murder Nathan to keep him from hurting your friend?"

She flinched, just the smallest amount. "I'd want to stop him from hurting her again, you mean." She inhaled deeply, her impressive bosom rising high. "I'd heard that he was guilty of far worse."

"Answer the question, if you please."

"Now that your friend has dug up the box, there's nothing more to hide. I certainly didn't murder anyone."

"Did you hire anyone?"

She seemed to be listening hard to a distant sound. "Oh dear. If you will excuse me?" She hurried out of the little room, and just as he was about to follow, she swiftly slammed the door shut and locked it.

He gave a deep sigh. The lady looked delicate, but she moved as fast as an adder. The situation wasn't dire, however. She'd left the key in the lock, and the door had a large gap at the bottom.

It didn't take him long to knock the key out of the lock and use one of the long pieces of silver he found in a drawer to drag the key under the door. He considered going back to the sitting room, grabbing Smith, and running to Weaver, but he didn't want to return to the village without answers.

When he found Mrs. Trout, she was just at the entrance to the kitchen, talking to one of the footmen. No doubt she was giving him instructions on how better to dispose of bodies next time.

"Stephen, good morning," Munro said as if they were passing in the street.

Stephen raised his eyebrows. "Sir?" he said. He didn't seem to have the air of a man who'd just slit someone's throat.

Mrs. Trout squeaked. She whirled around and glared at him.

"Yes, I escaped from the pantry. Now we will talk, if you please, ma'am. I won't brandish any knives or guns, though I have both on my person. Let's join Mr. Smith and Miss Trout in the sitting room and discuss this like civilized humans."

"Very well." She turned to Stephen. "Please accompany us. I do not trust Sir Civilized Person. He's trying to blame us for a murder."

Stephen wet his lips. He looked down at his shoes. Not so innocent after all.

As they walked past a window in the kitchen, Munro looked out and saw something. Or rather he noticed the lack of something.

"What the devil? Weaver's horse is gone. I left her tied to that post next to the stable yard."

"Ah. Mr. Weaver's horse?" Mrs. Trout said. "Not one of ours?"

"Oh no." Stephen peered out the window. "That must be the animal Mr.—"

Mrs. Trout cut him off with a loud "Hush."

But by then, Munro had figured it out. The footman would call only one servant Mister and the only other males in the house were servants. "Reed. The man Miss Trout referred to as 'yours.' Wait. Of course that means he came with you from London."

Her brows puckered in a pretense of confusion. "I don't understand what you're trying to say."

"It's very simple. I believe the butler did it."

"Just moments ago, you said you wished to return to the sitting room," she urged. "Shall we? Please."

He rubbed the bridge of his nose with thumb and forefinger. He hadn't had enough sleep the night before, and he had been shoved around by more emotion than he could recall suffering through in his life.

"I must go after Reed."

"He left at least ten minutes ago," Stephen said unconvincingly.

"And I don't know which direction he took," she said.

"Mrs. Trout, I haven't been as clever as I should have been, but even I know how to answer that. Tell me where Matilda Neely Smith has gone, and I suspect I know where he is."

Someone was calling his name, urgent and low, a man unable to add much volume to his voice.

"Smith," Munro shouted, then pushed past Stephen to find Joshua. That niggling doubt he'd had about Smith's innocence must have gone deep, because his sense of relief almost overwhelmed him.

"What's wrong?" he said when they met in the dining room.

"I thought you'd gone into it with someone," Smith said. "I heard a ruction and ruckus."

"Mrs. Trout locked me in the butler's pantry, probably to stop me from going after Reed."

"The butler?"

"Yes."

"Reed. You think he snuffed Nathan's candle, then? Do we know for sure?"

"Not yet." He gripped Smith's shoulder, the closest touch to an embrace he'd risk. "We'll be on our way soon."

Smith nodded.

They ended up in the sitting room once more. Munro pulled out his book and began to scribble a note.

Miss Trout still knitted and didn't seem interested in anything other than the yarn in her lap.

Stephen and the other footman, Dick, stood at attention at the door. But Munro had gathered the various weapons so they didn't present a threat—or so he hoped.

Munro paused in writing. "Why has Reed not been present during our previous visits?"

"He's a busy man." Mrs. Trout sneered at him. He wondered if she'd learned that from her sister-in-law.

"Was he afraid Smith might recognize him? Was he a Neely man?"

"Not at all." Mrs. Trout now attempted stiff and self-righteous. "He worked with me at the theater. A very efficient doorman there."

"And he got to know Miss Neely through you?"

Her shoulders drooped as the starch left her. Or she was trying another act on him? She rubbed her mouth. "I think we need tea. Stephen, please ring for some. Cook must be back by now."

"The bellpull works now?" Smith said.

"Yes. Of course. At second thought, Stephen and Dick, please go fetch it. We shall be fine. I don't expect any more trouble from Sir Ross or Mr. Smith. They know we're innocent of wrongdoing."

Munro held up the note he'd written. "Dick, go into town and deliver this to Constable Weaver."

The footman took the note but glanced at Mrs. Trout, who nodded. With a great gusty sigh, she pronounced, "We will cooperate."

"Now that Reed's off safely, that's hardly a surprise," Munro muttered to Smith.

The two servants left the room.

"Go on, Mrs. Trout. Here is your chance to explain."

He expected she would puff up and refuse, but she began to speak low and fast, as if getting a great load out of her system. Perhaps the latest shift in her manner had been genuine. He hoped so.

"Reed has a son named Matthew, who fell in love with Matilda Neely. They called each other Matty and planned to marry. So you see. He, ah, Reed senior, cares for Matilda. He thought of her as a daughter."

"I think I understand."

"Our old butler died soon after my dear Mr. Trout succumbed. I asked Reed to come here and work for me. He did and left his son Matty behind in London to work at the theater."

"And Reed Junior maintained some sort of relationship with Miss Neely."

"Yes. I don't know how they sneaked about, but they did. A few months back, Matty wrote to his father. Since Reed can't read—I think his eyes are failing and he refuses to get glasses—he asked me to read the letters he got. Most of them were gossipy fun notes about our old friends in London."

"When I was a gel, I was told one shouldn't gossip with the servants," Miss Trout interrupted dreamily. "I believe I missed out on many interesting stories because of that."

Munro waited, but she had nothing else to add. "Go on, please, Mrs. Trout."

"In the letter, Matty informed his father that his Matilda was expecting, which should have been a reason for joy. They weren't married yet, but it's not so strange for such things to happen. They were planning to sneak away and be married when her father's back was turned. But the day she managed to go meet Matty, she had burst into tears and confessed that the baby might not be his. She'd been drunk one night—been made drunk, I suspect—and had been taken by some of her father's men. Reed and Matty knew exactly who those men were. They accompanied her when they came to the theater."

She fell silent and stared out the window.

"Go on," Munro said.

"Matty was angry and hurt. He let her go, but then when he pulled his head out of his…when he realized what he'd done, he hurried to Mr. Neely's place of business and asked about his daughter. He got a good drubbing for his efforts. A terrible beating that nearly killed him, even though he didn't say a word about his intentions for Matilda or his possible, ah, part in her delicate condition. As he was so badly beaten, he learned she was to be married. He was told she'd be given to someone who'd keep her in line. Matty fled London and came here to recover from his injuries."

"And did Matthew get Matilda to come here as well?"

"I'm not sure. I think she figured out where he'd gone. She's a smart girl, our Matilda."

"Yes, such a dear gel." Miss Trout nodded in agreement.

"She said her father might guess where she'd fled because that terrible Nathan knew about my friendship with her. And she didn't want to leave us in danger, so after the baby was born, she left us, leaving behind the books and some of the money she'd taken. She said that the information in the books could destroy her father and it would be up to us to decide what to do. If we didn't want to deal with it, we could send it back to her father. Reed said he'd take care of the whole thing. He's the one who buried the box."

"She kept some of the money she stole?" Munro asked.

"Good," Smith muttered. He wore a bright smile, as if he'd gotten the best sort of news. "It'd be her dowry, then."

"Why would Reed kill Nathan rather than give him the message to take back to Neely?"

Mrs. Trout folded her arms, then unfolded them. Then she bowed her head, as if ceding control to Munro. "Reed has a temper."

Munro tried to remain patient but his "Go on" came out more stridently than it should have.

"He was arrested more than once in London for dustups. Any time anyone from London and the police were to show up, he'd hide himself away—in case he knew them. That is why he didn't serve you."

"He had good reason if he'd attacked Nathan and planned to do it again."

"Yes, Nathan. I thought Reed had gotten less ferocious with age, but... Understand, he is very fond of Matilda." She fiddled with a bracelet, the first untheatrical tic she'd shown. "He told me he'd gone after Nathan that first time. I'd hoped that redheaded fool had left the area after Reed's attack. I gather that Reed also hoped to do some violence to you, Mr. Smith. Because you took his son's place and married dear Matilda. But he tried the once, and you toppled him. And after that you were always with Sir Ross."

Smith's toothy smile showed, but this time his eyes remained cold. "He hoped to cut my throat too, you mean?"

She held out her hands in a theatrical entreaty—the heroine's pose as she seeks understanding or forgiveness in the final act of the drama, Munro suspected. "I think he...he might have meant not to murder you? He went after you next to the inn, after all, and people had seen him there last night."

"He got Nathan next to a busy market."

She let her hands drop. "I still believe he only wished to use you to carry a message. He-he knew your family and the Neelys too. He wanted the message to get to them that there'd be no more nonsense aimed at his family or mine."

"You agreed with his plan?"

"I abhor violence." She pressed her lips together and didn't say more.

"I don't," Miss Trout volunteered.

Stephen appeared with a tray holding saucers, teacups, and a teapot.

A few months ago, Munro would have put down his foot and insisted on getting answers from Miss and Mrs. Trout, trying to uncover their culpability in this crime, but Becky and his time in London had changed him into someone who saw more shades of gray. He only said, "Tea would be most welcome."

After all, getting the answers here would be someone else's job.

"And when you return to London?" Mrs. Trout asked after they'd been served cups of tea by Miss Trout.

"I'm not saying a thing to my father," Smith volunteered at once.

"And I shall make my report of her death entirely believable to her father," Munro said.

"What will you say to Constable Weaver?"

"I will tell him about Reed, but I don't expect that we need to mention anything of Mrs. Smith to Mr. Weaver."

Joshua Smith's smile at him made his heart beat faster, and he couldn't stop himself from donning a fatuous smile right back.

"We should take a photograph of her gravestone," Munro said. "It is rather convincing. I'll carry it back to her father."

Miss Trout muttered about trusting villainous men, but otherwise didn't object to their plan.

When Weaver came galloping up to the house, Munro went out to meet him.

It took only a few minutes to tell him about Reed and the way he'd fled the area. No one mentioned the fact that Mrs. Smith was still alive.

Weaver appeared far more upset about the missing horse than the missing murderer.

"Naturally, I shall reimburse you for the cost of the mare," Mrs. Trout said.

Weaver wore his impressive scowl. "Begging your pardon, ma'am, is that an admission of guilt for your part in the murder?"

She gave a tinkling laugh. "Of course not. It is a grateful widow helping the constabulary the best she is able."

Mrs. Trout had regained her aplomb; perhaps she was even more lighthearted because she was apparently getting away with something like a crime. Or perhaps it was relief because the problem of Matilda Smith was out of her hands.

Munro's earlier relief that he hadn't misjudged Smith still lingered and made him smile easily.

Even Weaver seemed less grim once he knew that he'd get a fleeter animal using Mrs. Trout's funds. He warned Mrs. Trout that she would have to give a statement, adding, "We will do what we can to find Reed."

He paused, and his frown deepened. Munro expected some stronger, angrier words for Mrs. Trout's part in allowing the murderous butler to escape. "I like Mr. Reed. He was a good cricketer, and we'll miss him on the team. But of course, we'll be sending along wires to the other boroughs and to Scotland Yard." He turned to Smith. "He'll be nabbed for murder, but I'll add your complaint of assault to his other charges, if you'd like?"

"No. I biffed him harder than he got me."

It was a surprisingly festive end to a murder investigation. Only the late Mr. Nathan of London might not agree.

***

Joshua and Munro walked away from Mrs. Trout's house. It was a glorious day of sun that actually spread warmth.

"What's that smell?" Joshua asked.

Munro stopped at the top of the hill and tilted his head back for a long breath. "Growing things. After a rainfall, even dirt smells like promise, eh?"

That seemed fanciful, but why not.

Promises. Joshua would give them and extract them, and he'd be free.

His wife was alive and well. Joshua already drafted letters in his head offering her congratulations and a divorce. He regretted not getting to know her, to be honest. She'd been brave, and shown him how easily a person could leave London and the entrapping arms of a family concern. If he wrote to her, he'd also add a bit about how he'd use his family and connections to keep Neely away from her should he discover the truth. Actually that might be the sort of news one didn't put in a letter. He commenced scheming.

Munro asked, "Why are you grinning like a demon?"

"I think I'll give a couple of those books of Neely's to my father. Maybe a couple of the jewels too."

"What? Why would you do that? You should send it along to Mrs. Smith. That's what Mrs. Trout thinks you're doing with the ones Weaver doesn't know about."

"Insurance."

"Explain yourself."

"My father understands the power of staying true to his word. I'll make him give his promise before I hand over anything. For power over Neely, he'll keep everyone away from the Trouts and from Matilda." He took his hat off and tucked it under his arm. The sun was too good not to feel on every part of him that it could reach.

Munro cleared his throat. "Add yourself too."

"Beg pardon?"

"Make your own freedom part of the condition before you hand over that tool. I'd say that so much leverage over his greatest…um, business foe means you could do even more. Get yourself out of his game as well."

"Me?"

"Yes, you, *mo laochain.*"

"What does that mean?"

"It's what we call wee brave lads."

"I'm hardly small." Joshua shot a glance at him and was pleased to note that Munro blushed.

Munro cleared his throat. "Indeed. But that is not the issue at hand."

Joshua guffawed. "Issue at hand," he explained.

"You are indeed childish. And you're avoiding the topic."

Joshua considered that possibility. "Perhaps."

"You seem to see yourself as in debt to your father. You might clear all debts."

It was Joshua's turn to redden. "Am I so obvious?"

"Only to someone who's been paying attention."

Any discomfort brought on by the mention of physical intimacy seemed mild compared to the effect of that warm comment, sincerely delivered.

When it came to this game of attempting to knock one another off mental balance, Munro would always win the contest. But Joshua could try another method.

"Ross," Joshua tried. It was a good name, short and easy, but with the suggestive hiss of air at the end.

Munro—Ross—smiled at him then. "Oh, I do like hearing you say that."

Joshua groaned. "Blimey. You win."

"I do?" Ross Munro blinked. "What do I win?"

"Me, for now," Joshua said.

Ross frowned a little. "The question is, what shall I do with you?"

"Anything you want."

Ross blushed.

That afternoon, they walked to the train station. Joshua sighed and looked down the tracks to the south. And then he looked north. He walked to the station master, who leaned against the wall, and asked when the northbound train would arrive. The man agreed to exchange his ticket.

Before they walked into the station, Ross called, "What are you doing?"

Joshua pointed north. He turned to the station master. "Be back in a mo'." He trotted over to Ross, who stood straight-backed and frowning, his jacket over one arm, his other hand clutching his carry-all.

"I'm having a change of plans. I thought I'd go see what the wilds of Scotland are like. I've heard they're pretty. And I do like the accent."

"You're daft. You can't just take off like... Like that."

"Like what? A creature sprung from a trap?" Joshua laughed out loud at the idea. Pure pleasure. "Why not? I'll send a letter to my father. Tell him what's what. Wait to hear back." He smiled. "Maybe on my way north, I'll stop off to see my wife, eh? Get to know the other person who helped spring me from that damned trap."

"You're a lunatic," Ross said, but he was smiling.

"Want to join me?"

Ross went silent. He shifted from foot to foot. Just then, smoke rose in the distance. The southbound train gave a warning cry they could hear a mile away.

He didn't look at Joshua and instead stared at the smoke. The moments passed, so long that Joshua felt as if his entire existence could have turned on them, the whole story changing with each puff of smoke Ross stared up at.

"I expect you need a guide," Ross said, apparently talking to the sky.

"Yes, I do. I'm barely used to being outside London."

"I can get Kelly to send me the money he owes me anywhere I end up."

"I say Scotland. The accent," Joshua reminded him. "Makes me excited."

Ross rolled his eyes.

"Excited about life," Joshua said. "And other things."

The train's brakes squealed as it slowed to enter the station. The great draft of the engine blew over them.

Ross turned and walked swiftly toward the brick building. "Come along, then. We'll both need to exchange our tickets," he called over his shoulder.

Joshua ran so quickly, his hat flew off. He leaned down, grabbed it up, and chased after his future.

The End

From His American Detective (book one of the Victorian Gay Detective series)

The sole survivor of his family's gruesome murder years earlier, "Poor Little Ned Lawton" has struggled to put the dark events behind him. So when a brash New York detective darkens his doorway demanding an interview, the wealthy young gentleman immediately shuts him out. But a rash of murders in America are mirroring of the London killings, and Patrick Kelly knows Ned might be the key to stopping the bloodshed.

Lawton, now called Edmund Sloan, is a wealthy young gentleman and philanthropist. He's spent most of his life pushing all memories of his old family and that horrific day from his thoughts. Now a brash, provocative American detective insists he dredge up the past.

Together, Patrick and the unwilling Edmund must uncover the truth of the murders before the killer strikes again, whether it is in New York or London. As they hunt down secrets from his past, Edmund can't hide his other secret from the sharp-eyed detective: the attraction he feels for men and the enticing Patrick in particular.

Excerpt…

Prologue

1874

Young Edmund overheard the murmurs from adults. He caught his old name: *Poor Little Ned…the only survivor…that hideous murder*. But then someone would immediately shush the conversation—usually Papa Sloan.

Only once during those early years did someone come right out and ask. In the school's refectory, a new student slid onto the polished bench next to Edmund and, after prayers, introduced himself as Wensler. He picked up his spoon and, between bites of soupy porridge asked, "You're truly Lawton? My mum told me you would be in my year. She said what happened to your family was in all the papers. Even though it was ages and ages ago."

Edmund's stomach squeezed tight. "Years ago."

"Want to hear what my mother told me?"

Edmund didn't want to know. He needed to know. He couldn't help himself—he nodded.

Wensler spoke with relish. "It all happened in the dining room, she told me."

Edmund waited, unable to eat another bite of lukewarm mush. He always had trouble eating at these long tables amongst the crowds of boys, in the air that smelled of burnt toast and sweat, but now his throat closed entirely. The students hadn't been dismissed from breakfast, so he couldn't run away from this conversation.

"The papers said the whole room was all over blood." Wensler, pale and skinny, had a wide mouth and restless hands that he used to build the scene in the air in front of him. "The bodies were on chairs pushed into the table. A grand table in a huge grand dining room. All set up like they were eating, but it was bits of their body they were eating. The eyes were all out."

Edmund couldn't move or speak. After a moment, Wensler went on. "I wager the article didn't say what parts they were eating. Do you know?"

Edmund shook his head.

"I suppose hands or feet?" Wensler gestured to his face and his too-wide mouth. "Shoved right down their throats."

Edmund had a fleeting glimpse of something even worse, so much worse, and he punched the boy hard on the shoulder to keep him from saying another word.

"Ow, hey," Wensler yelped. Up and down the table, chatter stopped and boys watched, amazed, for Edmund was the best-behaved boy in the school. Despite the attack, Wensler didn't lunge at Edmund. No teachers had seen the incident, and Wensler didn't report Edmund.

That was the end of the matter.

Except not entirely, for during his next holiday, Edmund made the mistake of going to the library and asking Papa Sloan about the bodies posed at the table. Papa Sloan carefully lowered the book he held. He stood and motioned to the door. "It's nothing for little boys to think of. You should go to your room now."

That cold disapproval added fuel to Edmund's bad dreams. He woke sweating and whimpering he'd lost another home. Never mind that he'd tried to be a perfect student, a perfect foster son—he'd failed. They would take him away, and he'd lose everything again.

That same holiday, on his last full day, he listened to another conversation—he had become adept at creeping about the house and eavesdropping—between Mother Sloan and her bosom friend. "One shall miss him when he returns to school. He is a quiet, agreeable child," she told her friend.

With that, Edmund became nearly happy. After he returned to school, he even sought out Wensler to beg his pardon for hitting him.

"But you don't want to tell me about the Dreadful Scene of the Terrible Murder?" Wensler asked, obviously disappointed.

A wave of nausea shook Edmund so he had trouble speaking. He forgot his agreeable nature. "If you talk about it again, I'll beat you senseless."

Within weeks, his lost family sank back into the past where it belonged, though several years later, he wondered if that event in his past had turned him into a deviant. But by then Edmund knew better than to express such troublesome thoughts to anyone, even his now-close friend, Wensler. He remained silent as the Lawtons' tomb.

Chapter One

Ten years later, London

The source of information in London had clammed up entirely, not even returning wire messages, so Patrick persuaded his boss at the inquiry agency to let him go find answers in person. The similarities in the murders had to be worth a trip overseas, he told Mr. Greene, and the agency's New York clients agreed.

If he were right, he'd prove himself to Mr. Greene. And maybe he'd get a chance to thumb his nose at the cops. Past time to put out the small fire of rage still burning inside him after his abridged career with the New York Police Department.

He got off the train from Liverpool and made his way to the London inquiry office without taking the time to look around the city. The British agent, a gray-haired man whose walrus-mustache ends dangled past his chin, sat behind his desk and didn't budge from the position he'd stated in his letter. "I have nothing more to report. The gentlemen in question refuse to see us."

"You won't even go to the house to request an interview from Edmund Lawton?" Patrick almost slipped and called him Poor Little Ned.

The ends of the man's mustache quivered and his round face flushed. "He is Mr. Sloan. He hasn't used that other name since he was a small child. And no, we sent a note and were refused. We will not take steps that'll seriously annoy him. Our company's standing is at risk. He or his foster father could persuade our clients we're unethical."

"God save you from the wrath of an irked wealthy man," Patrick said. "He won't invite you to his next dinner party."

Patrick said good-bye and left before the man had an apoplectic fit.

Since he didn't have any appointments until the next day, Patrick went to a library to discover more about the horrible murders from the past—stories from this side of the ocean. And he was direly curious why the two Mr. Sloans wielded so much power in society. He didn't find anything new. The foster father, a lawyer, had appeared in newspaper stories and society columns, attending all sorts of highfalutin events until he'd grown ill a year ago.

The younger Sloan had always been a recluse and was rarely mentioned in those endless lists of party-goers. Lawton/Sloan apparently belonged to a number of clubs and was on all sorts of committees. Neither seemed the kind of men to break legs if things didn't go their way. But what did Patrick know of wealthy men? Maybe they dispatched their enemies as often as dockworkers, but with more finesse and discretion.

The next morning, he took the time to be a tourist only long enough to walk several miles from his hotel to the home of Mr. Edmund Sloan, born Ned Lawton, a man only two years Patrick's senior, who had spent more money on just this one London address than Patrick would earn in his lifetime. And, ha, the man had another house in the country.

Sloan had lived through hell but now lived in paradise, if a looming townhouse in London fit anyone's version of heaven.

Every inch of Lawton/Sloan's small corner of the city seemed to have been scrubbed clean by an army of servants. Even the potted topiary trees out front of the carved granite steps didn't have a polished leaf out of place.

Poor little rich boy, Patrick thought as he slapped the gleaming brass knocker against the sky-blue door. A guy in tails answered the door. Patrick's very first real English butler. He snapped the man a salute. "I'm here to see Mr. Sloan."

The butler didn't look him up and down, nothing so vulgar. His gaze flickered, though. "What name shall I give?"

"I'm Mr. Kelly, late of New York, on an official investigation." In his old life, he would have pulled out his badge, but he worked for Mr. Greene's private company now and had nothing to show other than a commanding air, which he hoped he could still manage.

"If you would leave your card, sir?"

"No, don't have one," he lied. "And tell him I can wait as long as it takes. I need to see him."

The butler led him into a huge room, all marble, dark wood, and a roaring fire. "Please wait here."

Alone, Patrick pulled off his hat and threw it on a chair. Why would he be allowed run of the house? And then he noticed a burly man standing in the corner, his feet shoulder width apart, his hands behind his back. He had the blank face of a cop or a vagrant, only with a better haircut.

Patrick wandered over. "My guess is you're a footman."

Still staring into the distance, the man gave a tiny nod.

"Ha! Wonderful. What's your name?"

"Liam, sir."

"Irish?"

Liam's mouth went thin, and for a moment, his eyes shifted to Patrick. "No sir."

Apparently even the question was an insult. Patrick's mother might give the man a good talking-to. As it was, Patrick felt the need to prod more, just for the sake of entertainment. He already knew that Mr. Sloan was a well-liked young man with many friends and no enemies, other than anyone who tried to talk to him about his past.

He gazed around at all the knickknacks and statues and thought about the man with no enemies. How had a man as rich as Sloan managed that?

Mr. Edmund Sloan gave to charity. He attended the opera, plays, musical fetes, dances, but he didn't sit down to dine with anyone, not even at his two clubs. Before they'd clammed up, the British inquiry agency had reported that Sloan must live on air.

Patrick asked Liam, "How do you like working for Mr. Sloan?"

"Fine, sir." Liam's gaze shifted to the door. He obviously longed for the butler to return and rescue him. Which, of course, made Patrick all the more interested in quizzing him.

"Have you been here long?"

"Three years, sir."

"Mr. Sloan is a good employer?"

"None better, sir."

"And the pay is good?"

Again the mouth went thin and the eyes grew cold. Patrick had been warned that talk of money was uncultured. "There are no positions open at the time," Liam said, showing real emotion at last. "And if you wanted to work for Mr. Sloan, you would apply to Mr. Becker, the butler, and enter through the side door, the servants' entrance."

That explained the sudden hostility. "Whoops. I'm here for Sloan, not Becker. But I'll keep your advice in mind." He wandered over to an ornate display case and examined the pottery behind the glass. It looked ugly to him, all giant blue and red and green Chinese things. On the mantel, a gold-and-china clock ticked, and a bulging-eyed silver cow stood next to that. Sloan might be wealthy, but his taste ran to froufrou junk.

He grabbed one of the heavier sculptures of a mother and child.

"This one is a tad nicer," he remarked to the footman. "Even though they look feeble-minded, the way they're goggling at each other."

Liam actually took a step forward. "Sir. That's a very valuable piece."

"Really." Patrick turned it over to examine its base. "Looks like something that I could win on the boardwalk at Coney Island."

"I have a Dalou, if you prefer something more modern." The cultured voice came from a man standing in the doorway. He and Patrick might be about the same age, but this man had scads more sophistication, which made him seem ancient in a way—timeless. Wealth at a glance at forty paces. The impression came from all the details added up: a fine gray suit, elegant hands, glossy dark hair, and a patronizing smirk.

"Please put that down," Mr. Supercilious said.

Patrick took another second to look at the sculpture—just to show he wasn't about to take orders. He needed this guy, though, and when he put the thing back on the mantel, he did so with care. He went to Sloan and stuck out his hand.

"Patrick Kelly from New York."

Sloan stared at his outstretched hand before at last giving it a short, firm shake. The strength in his fingers surprised Patrick. Then Sloan took a step away and put his hands at his back. Did he avoid touch, or had he been trained to use parade rest?

"Why are you here in London, Mr. Kelly?" Mr. Sloan's directness suited Patrick just fine.

"To see you, Mr. Sloan," he said. He dropped his voice. "Or, I should say, Mr. Lawton."

Patrick appreciated the way the man fought surprise and nearly won—a fast pucker of eyebrows, a mouth squeezed tight. Sloan had nothing on the butler when it came to hiding emotion.

Sloan must have sent some signal behind his back, because the footman crossed the room and left, closing the door silently behind him.

Patrick tensed when the expression on Sloan's face shifted to something more vivid—the dark eyes filled with anger. The illustrations Patrick had seen of Poor Ned Lawton from years ago had caught the shape of those eyes, rimmed by lashes almost as extravagant as the boy had had. That must have been a nuisance for him with other boys.

"How much do you want?" Sloan asked.

"Huh?"

"To keep your mouth closed. How many pounds? No doubt some dreadful publication has set you on my trail, but I'll pay more to kill the story. What's your price? And I'll add a bonus if you give me your publisher's name."

About the Author

Summer Devon is the alter ego of Kate Rothwell. Kate/Summer lives in Connecticut, USA, and also writes books, usually gaslight historicals, as Kate.

For more information about Summer and Kate, go to http://katerothwell.com or http://summerdevon.com. Summer can also be found at https://www.facebook.com/S.DevonAuthor

Look for these titles by Summer Devon

Solitary Shifter series:
Taming the Bander
Revealing the Beast
Releasing the Shifter

Single title

The Private Secretary
The Gentleman and the Lamplighter
Sibling Rivals
Goodbye Phillip
Tail of the Dog
Goodbye Phillip
Must Loathe Norcross
The Hanged Man's Hero
Hot Under the Collar
The Hanged Man's Hero
His American Detective

Titles written with Bonnie Dee

Seducing Stephen
The Gentleman and the Rogue
The Nobleman and the Spy
Sin and the Preacher's Son
The Psychic and the Sleuth
The Gentleman's Keeper
The Gentleman's Madness
Mending Him
The Bohemian and the Banker

***Victorian Holiday Hearts series*:**
Simon and the Christmas Spirit
Will and the Valentine Saint
Mike and the Spring Awakening

Summer Devon

Delaney and the Autumn Masque

Titles Written as Kate Rothwell
(m/f romance)

Somebody Wonderful
Somebody to Love
Someone to Cherish
Thank You, Mrs. M
Seducing Miss Dunaway (free novella)
Protecting Miss Samuels
Powder of Sin
Her Mad Baron
Love Between the Lines
Mademoiselle Makes a Match
The Earl, a Girl, and a Promise

Printed in Great Britain
by Amazon

43039886R00121